BEHIND
CROOKED SMILES

ANN BAYAH

Printed in the United States of America

First Printing, 2015

ISBN 978-0-615-88443-1

Dedication

This book is dedicated to everyone who's ever had the experience of having a dream deferred, to everyone who read FRAC-TURED and needed closure on some matters, and finally to everyone who has supported my efforts to bring the fictional Mitchell family to life on the pages within.

Special gratitude to George my editor, Ed Towles my illustrator, and Jesse my formatter. Without your collective business acumen and level of professionalism, I could not have published this book.

1

It's an uphill climb to the bottom when your spirit's gone missing. As Lindie lay curled up on her bed, Easter Monday 1965 was serving to be nothing more than an empty vessel for feelings of regret and anger to flow into. Over and over again she asked herself how her plan could have gone so wrong. Just the day before, she had so much hope, fortified by a keen determination to embark upon a new life away from Fullerton, Maryland. Now, less than twenty-four hours later, she was in a state of depression triggered by her foiled attempt to run away. Her initial punishment was to serve a parental-imposed sentence of isolation even though it was a day off from school. She had been sequestered in her bedroom, not allowed to play with her sisters, not allowed to watch TV, not allowed to talk on the telephone, and worst yet, not allowed to write in her journal. The journal had been confiscated—by which parent she did not know. She feared (Ruby) her mother, in warrior mode, would appear in the doorway of her bedroom at any moment to announce that arrangements had been made for her to be sent off to reform school. If such were to happen, Lindie's desire to escape the self-defined demons of her childhood would fizzle away like an Alka Seltzer tablet plopped into a glass of water.

Lindie repeatedly punched her tear-soaked pillow in anger. She looked across her room and saw her untouched, skimpy breakfast of cold toast and orange juice. She had no appetite. Vinnie, her youngest sister, had brought the tray in earlier and asked, "What's gonna happen to you, Lindie, and why'd you want to leave us? If you leave, who's gonna help me and Francine make mud pies and push the wagon around the yard?"

"I'm not supposed to talk to you, remember; so put the tray down and leave me alone."

That was earlier, but Lindie continued to languish in her sorrow long after that exchange with her baby sister.

* * *

I could die in here, having choked on a piece of toast, but who would really care? Maybe I could sneak to the bathroom, grab a bottle of aspirin, and swallow them with the glass of orange juice. I hate living where people barely tolerate my family and probably call us all kinds of names behind our backs. If it weren't for tavern customers, hardly anybody would talk to us. Some snooty family members don't. Cousin Drusilla and her family have never set foot in our house. I need to live somewhere else. And why did I have to be the oldest daughter? If I were Vinnie's age, I'd be too young to understand the way things are around here. I'd live out each day blind to the reality of being a member of the Mitchell family in a place like Fullerton on the outskirts of nowhere.

Gradually Lindie's negative brain chatter quieted, and she fell asleep again while thinking about what took place after her father (Theo) interrupted her dream opportunity at Aunt Nita's back door. Had some act of fate sent her father outside to smoke a cigar at that exact moment? Then there was the shouting as his inflamed query awakened everyone in the house in the aftermath of her bold attempt to run away.

* * *

Seconds after she had initiated her attempt to escape and stepped through Aunt Nita's back door, Lindie's world morphed into a theatrical tragedy. What followed was a confrontation on a scale she could not have imagined. She came face to face with her father.

As Theo slammed the back door shut, he yelled, "I asked you where the hell you thought you was goin'?

Instead of immediately responding to her father's question, Lindie bit down on her bottom lip and glared at the floor. A sudden onset of fright as she had never known took control of her brain. Never, ever had her father been so upset with her. She could not look at him. Being caught was not something she had factored into her escape plan; everyone was supposed to have been asleep, clearing her path for a smooth get-a-way to a new life.

"I asked you a question!"

Tears emerged from Lindie's eyes in the form of large droplets as she finally managed to yell out, "Away!"

Before she could continue, Cousin Alvin joined the scene. He hadn't even taken time to put on his slippers, opting to race down the back stairs clad in his striped green and beige pajamas, sporting an elf-like matching cap, "What the blue blazes is going on down here?"

"I caught her tryin' to run away."

"Run away? You must be mistaken." Alvin then turned his attention to Lindie, "Why are you up at this hour, doodle?"

Lindie's worst nightmare was about to get worse. Her mother entered the kitchen before Lindie could offer a response to her cousin. "What's all this racket down here?"

"Yo' daughter was 'bout to run off."

Ruby brushed past Alvin, and spat out with exaggerated disgust, "Say what?"

"You heard me. I was sittin' outside havin' a smoke, and guess who came tippin' out the back door like a thief?" Theo snatched Lindie's crumbled paper sack from her hand and held it up high. "See her fancy suitcase."

Lindie started a loud wailing cry as her hands shielded her face. Ruby was poised to attack, but Alvin intervened by stepping in to comfort his little cousin. "Don't cry doodle. We can fix whatever is going on here." A split second later, Ruby yanked

Alvin away from Lindie and confronted her.

"Surely you've lost your mind this time. How dare you bring this kind of shame on our family? This tops everything else you've ever pulled out of your bag of stunts. Get your too grown behind back upstairs, and I'm coming up there and give you a whipping you'll remember til the day you die." Ruby grabbed Lindie by the arms, forcing her toward the stairs. "Soon as we get back home, we're gonna see about sending you away to reform school. Maybe they can get rid of the devil in you."

Instead of climbing the stairs, Lindie pulled away from her mother and fixed an evil glare on her face. "I'll gladly go to reform school because I wouldn't have to be around you."

Faster than a cobra's strike, Ruby raised a fist and knocked her daughter across the face. The powerful blow sent Lindie flying across the arm of the sofa and onto the floor along with a lamp from an end table. Alvin and Theo grabbed Ruby by her arms before she could render another blow.

"Ruby, calm down before one of our neighbors calls the police!"

"Let go of me!" Ruby then ordered Lindie back to bed. "Get upstairs like I said. You're really gonna get it now!"

By then everyone else in the house was watching either from the landing of the stairs or from the steps, including Marvin (Theo's stuttering alcoholic brother) who shared, "I-I-I can't sleep wid all thisss noise."

As Lindie rose from the floor and began to climb the stairs, Uncle Jimmie, with his wife Aunt Nita clinging to him, stated, "I don't know how this got started, but I'm not going to stand for this kind of trashy behavior in my house. We're God-fearing people not heathens."

"Oh Mother and Father, I'm afraid one of our little doodles is having a problem, but we're going to fix everything when day breaks. Everybody should go back to bed and settle their nerves," pleaded Alvin.

Ruby was not ready to be silenced.

"The absolute gall of her to try and run away and while we're visiting relatives. You've embarrassed me for the last time. I regret the day you were . . . ."

That nearly vile and partially stated comment from her mother was the line Lindie just could not let go. She had been holding it in too tightly and for too long. The anger within was a motivating force when she stopped midway on the stairs. Her sobbing ceased and as though propelled by sheer determination or the need for revenge, she looked directly at her mother. Lindie's anger had shifted from startup to full throttle, and she fired a verbal shot intended to seriously wound, "What do you regret, Momma . . . the day I was born?" It was as though she was having an out-of-body experience as she continued, "You can't keep blaming getting pregnant with me as the reason you married a man you didn't love." The words slid past her lips so fast, there wasn't even a pause to think how best to string the sentence together, but once a shot is fired, it can't be taken back. Things had happened too fast for anyone to have intervened further at that point.

An immediate and audible gasp from everyone was followed by what must have been a collective sense of *Oh My God.* For a second, the room fell silent as Ruby locked eyes with her husband. Everyone else's eyes darted back and forth between the distressed mother and daughter. For what seemed like a string of seconds, only a selection of Alvin's faint and haunting classical music filled the air.

"Why you little snot!" Ruby lunged toward Lindie, but Theo grabbed Ruby's robe and pulled her back.

"We not gonna be actin' like our ignorant neighbors up in here; you two done lost yo' minds?"

The would-be run-a-way turned and ran up the remaining steps while Theo struggled to keep his wife from approaching the stairs. Everyone was surprised by what Lindie had just alluded to —an unexpected dark secret with the potential to unravel a family. The adults appeared to be in a state of shock. Their initial reactions almost replicated a slow-motion scene in a silent movie— hands to mouths and looks of unspeakable dismay.

Then it was Aunt Nita's turn at attempting to restore peace and calm. With a shaky voice she declared, "The Lord don't like ugly, and this seems real ugly to me. Everybody should go back to bed and stop this fighting. Ruby, you know you weren't brought up to act like this. I'm ashamed of you."

A perplexed Theo responded while still holding onto his wife, "Aunt Nita, I don't mean no disrespect, but we ain't goin' back to bed, cause we leavin'. Ruby, get dem girls things packed up, and the Fullerton crowd is goin' the hell home."

"It's 3 o'clock in the morning," reminded Ruby as Alvin re-
acted with disbelief.

"You heard me, woman! Get dem girls packed up."

Lindie's sisters had been standing on the landing as well, peer-
ing through the railings of the banister, but when their father
stated they were going back home, they ran back to the room
they had been sleeping in. Even they understood that the Easter
visit had turned into something really bad, and in their minds, it
was all their big sister's fault.

"Now hold on a minute, Theo. I don't think you all should be
leaving in the middle of the night like this. Feelings are too raw
right now; go back to bed like Nita said and sleep on this. Whatever this is about, we can talk it over in the morning when everybody's got a clear head," suggested Uncle Jimmy.

"I don't care what time it is, I said we leavin', and I ain't
waitin' for nobody to get dressed. I'm gonna start the car up,
Ruby. Whoever ain't in the car in ten minutes will be left. If you
don't believe it, try me. Marvin, you better get yo' gitty-up in
gear too."

Ruby shot a disgusted look at her husband before he yelled for
the would-be run-a-way, "Lindie, get down here; you're goin' to
the car wid me right now!"

"Oh dear, this is so unfortunate," lamented Alvin as he picked
up the overturned lamp and flopped down on the sofa with his
head in his hands.

As Theo reached the front door, Lindie joined him, and he

paused to address his hosts. Ruby had whipped past Lindie and was upstairs hurriedly packing.

"Uncle Jimmie, Aunt Nita, Alvin, I'm so sorry 'bout all this, but as you can see, we got a huge problem to deal wid. Lindie, you goin' to the car wid me cause I don't want you upstairs wid yo' momma."

Alvin addressed Theo again, "We just need for everybody to take a deep breath and relax. Theo, I have some nice brandy if you'd like a shot. There must be an explanation for this."

"Don't want no brandy, and right now I don't care 'bout no explanation, so like I said, we leavin'. We need to fix this at home, not in somebody else's house."

After gathering her youngest two girls, Ruby offered her deepest apologies to her aunt and uncle and ushered them back to bed, promising everything was under control, and she'd fill in details later—maybe.

However, Alvin was still in a tizzy, "Let me pack up some ham sandwiches for you all. I can't believe this is happening. She seemed fine last night. What could have happened in the span of a few hours to make her want to run away and God forbid in a city she doesn't know to boot?"

"I ain't no Einstein, but seems like somethin' been festerin' fo' a while. Don't make no big fuss over us; I don't think nobody's got food on their minds."

"Did you . . . did you and Ruby really have a shotgun wedding?" asked Alvin.

"Weren't no gun held to my head." Theo then addressed

Lindie. "Maybe yo' momma's got somethin' she needs to tell me after all des years. What you almost said . . . I ain't even gonna ask where you got that notion from."

Lindie looked down at the floor while rubbing the arm that had braced her fall earlier. Certainly if she were to tell her father about the old love letters—hell fire would consume her.

Alvin dashed into the kitchen where he quickly wrapped up sandwiches as Wagner's "The Ride of the Valkyries" chimed on.

Within the time frame set by Theo, the car from Fullerton was loaded with disheartened passengers. Theo issued an order as he pulled away from the house where a wicked fury had just played out. "Let me tell ya'll somethin', if even one person starts up durin' this ride home, I'm gonna pull this car over and put you out. I ain't makin' no bathroom stops—nothin', so don't even part yo' lips to ask." With that said, he made a left turn and skidded away. The only sounds heard during the ride back to Fullerton were the hum of the car's engine and the occasional passing vehicles. Ruby spent most of the ride staring out of the window into the darkness. The lid of her Pandora's Box had been cracked, and a secret from long ago would likely be revealed.

With the exception of Ruby and Lindie, the passengers quickly fell asleep. Lindie kept her head lowered and repeatedly scolded herself for blurting out something that would guarantee punishment on a scale she had likely never known. *Why couldn't I have been born into a normal family? Now I've spoiled Easter for everybody.* Trying to imagine the extent of her punishment kept her mind occupied for the rest of the ride.

2

The Mitchells arrived back in Fullerton around 6 a.m., before dawn. Theo unlocked the tavern and told Marvin to wait inside until he could drive him to the bus depot for his return trip to Baltimore.

"Ruby, fix dem girls some toast and juice, and I want all ya'll to go to bed—no fussin' no nothin'. Lindie, don't come outta yo' room till I tell you to. Vinnie'll bring you some food."

"I need to go to the bathroom," whined Lindie.

"Me too," said Vinnie.

"Okay, bathroom and then off to bed. Ruby, I'm a bring the bags in and then meet me back at the car after you get dem in bed."

The moment Ruby had dreaded for years had perhaps arrived. Her husband was going to question her about a secret she had closely guarded, and she had no rehearsed explanation to offer.

The facts had been locked in the back of her mind for so long, having been shared with no one. She quietly chided herself, wondering why after all of this time, the truth had to surface and possibly thrust her into a new reality. Possibilities raced through her mind, but in the end she surmised that before their old home burned to the ground, Lindie must have unearthed the love letters she had written to another man. As a tension headache throbbed at her left temple, she felt tremendous guilt for having held onto the letters even though J had been killed in a car accident three years earlier. Even he had not known the truth, but a fact known to most women is that a first love is never really forgotten. A place in the heart remains theirs forever, so Ruby kept the letters as mementos of what once was.

Theo was waiting outside, but Ruby lingered in the living room after she had gotten her youngest two in bed. Despite the years that had passed, she let thoughts of J fill her mind--his smell, his touch, and most of all how the firmness of his body melted into hers when two friends finally became lovers. He had awakened feelings she could not control. She shook her head from side to side as the memory of those experiences competed with her stress headache. Their friendship had elevated to passion weeks before she became Mrs. Theodore Mitchell. In all the years of her marriage to Theo, there had been no moments of mind-blowing pleasure for her in the bedroom. She had often wondered if other married women suffered a nullification of physical bliss with their husbands. Women she knew never talked about their bedroom experiences because it was a highly taboo subject.

She thought about Mrs. Webster and her husband Otha. With his grossly overweight body and rotten teeth, what was he doing for his wife? Smiles and jovial demeanors likely covered up lots of heartache and disappointment in lots of relationships.

"Ruby!" Theo's call interrupted his wife's contemplative reflections.

Ruby placed one foot in front of the other and exited the house worried about how the talk with her husband would turn out. As written by Kahlil Gibran, "For life goes not backwards . . . ." but at that moment, she wanted more than anything to be catapulted back to a more innocent time.

"You and me is goin' fo' a ride. Get in!"

"We gonna leave the girls here alone?"

"Quit stallin' and get in the damn car!"

They rode in silence as Theo barreled down Back Creek Road until he pulled into a dirt path that both were familiar with. He parked at the ferry crossing. Ripples of churning water could be heard splashing against the bank of the river. The area was sometimes used as a hide-a-way for lovers in parked cars. While it offered solitude, being so close to the river's edge in the semi-darkness meant approaching with caution since there was no barrier between the dirt path and the water. When Ruby and Theo were courting, they had only frequented the location during daylight hours in order to watch fishing boats go by. Those were indeed happier times.

A half-moon was sliding behind the clouds, and although the surface of the water looked serene before the light of dawn, serenity did not define the current mood of the couple parked at the water's edge.

After taking a deep breath, Theo got out of the car and slammed the door hard enough to rock the vehicle. Ruby remained in the car wringing her hands while her husband paced back and forth like a caged tiger with his hands shoved into his back pockets. Then he stopped at the front door on the passenger's side of the car and swung it open.

"Get out!"

"It's chilly out there. Can't we talk in the car?"

"I said get out!"

Ruby released a heavy sigh and eased her feet onto the sandy ground just inches from her husband. She was nervous but not afraid of him. There had never been a physical altercation between the two of them in all the years they had been married. However, Ruby knew that once her husband was really upset, he would argue his point until he wore down anyone who opposed his view. On that early morning, she was the opposition.

"I been thinkin' on this since we left Dearmount, so give it to me straight. What did Lindie mean by what she said at Aunt Nita's?"

Ruby hung her head and shuffled her feet. "I don't know where to begin."

"Start wid the truth! Was I a fool? Was you messin' 'round wid some other guy while we was courtin'?"

"I never thought of you as a fool."

"Out wid it, Ruby! What was the girl talkin' 'bout? "

"Apparently Lindie found some old . . . old love letters I had kept."

"I ain't never wrote you no love letters."

"I'm well aware of that fact. They were from the person I was seeing before you and I got married."

"Love letters? Yo' daddy told me you wasn't seein' nobody."

"I had planned to tell my parents, but Daddy had his heart set on you becoming his son-in-law. He kept inviting you over to our house hoping I'd take a liking to you. Momma and Daddy didn't know that I liked someone who was away at college."

"Well he sure as hell wasn't from Fullerton cause ain't nobody from here been to no college. I wanna know if he's got anythin' to do wid you and me now. Do I know him?"

"He lived in Brookville, and you wouldn't have known him. He didn't want to be called junior, so he went by J."

"What'da you mean he lived? When was the last time you saw him?"

Ruby knew that answering this question could possibly end her marriage or at least change her relationship with Theo forever. "Theo, it was a long time ago. We don't have to rehash this now."

"Oh yes we do. Keep talkin'."

Despite the harm that her answer would render, she confessed to a portion of a hidden truth, "He and I were close a couple of times before you and I got married."

"You and me was goin' steady for at least four-five months befo' we got married. You mean to tell me you was two-timin' me all that time?"

"Not exactly."

"What exactly? Sounds like two-timin' to me."

"He was away in college and only came home now and then. We exchanged letters mostly. When he found out I was about to be married, he took a Greyhound to Brookville and hitch-hiked to Fullerton."

"So, I guess he didn't do all that travelin' and hitch-hikin' just to shake yo' hand?"

"He was so upset. It was the last time we were together. He begged me to elope with him, but I couldn't, so he went back to Virginia alone. I had promised to marry you. Daddy would have tracked me down, and you would have looked like a fool once word got out that your bride-to-be had run off with another man."

"Don't act like you did me some favor, cause I sure feel like a fool standin' here listenin' to my wife tellin' me she laid down with another man but married me out of pity. Where is this J man now?"

"You don't have to worry about him interfering in our marriage because he died three years ago in a car accident."

Theo grabbed Ruby by the shoulders and yelled just inches from her face, "You married me fo' all the wrong reasons, Ruby! Did you ever love me?"

Ruby lowered her head and muttered, "I did have feelings for you."

Theo released her shoulders with such force that she almost lost her footing.

"Feelin's . . . lucky me. So everythin' you said at the altar before God and all the guests was a lie . . . Died three years ago you say, ain't that convenient, but you kept his love letters . . . is this a lie too? Is he really livin' somewhere close by and you've been sneakin' off to see him?"

"No, he's really dead."

"Theo grabbed Ruby by her shoulders again and forced her to look directly at him. "Tell me this, Ruby, why the lie? You could 'a told yo' father you didn't love me. What was goin' on in yo' head?"

Ruby exhaled slowly before she answered. "I wanted a husband."

"You could 'a eloped and married J.

"No, he was dead set on finishing his last two years of college."

"So what was the rush to get married?"

Ruby broke loose from her husband's grip and turned her back on him.

"Wait a minute . . . Lawd, don't let this be what I'm thinkin'; was you expectin' a baby?"

Through trembling lips, she confessed, "Yes, I was expecting."

"Well I'll be damn! I hadn't touched you befo' we got married. You was actin' all sanctified and like. What did you do, go to some hack and got rid of the baby?"

"No, I didn't get rid of the baby."

Dawn had crept in when Theo stepped in front of his wife and glared at her for a second; then he responded in shock, "Lindie? All this is 'bout that other man being her father, not me? You said she was born early."

Ruby raised her voice and blurted out the other half of her hidden truth, "You're not her father!"

Ruby could see the hurt and bewilderment on her husband's face. For a split second she thought that maybe for the first time he was going to strike her. Instead, Theo moved to the front of the car and slammed both of his fists onto the hood three times yelling at the top of his lungs, "Go-o-d-dammit, god-dammit, god-dammit! You knew you was gonna have a baby when you married me. I was a blind fool then, and I've been a fool all des years."

"I didn't know what else to do. I was afraid to try and end the pregnancy. It was too close to our wedding day when I found out. What if something had gone wrong? Then everybody would have known. I didn't think of you as a fool."

"Like hell you didn't. I made an honest woman outta you and kept you from bringin' shame on yo' family. Go-o-damn! Who else knew? Did you tell this J-man?"

"I didn't tell him. I was so scared; I couldn't tell anybody. I felt so ashamed. Momma and Daddy would have been embarrassed, and you wouldn't have married me. I wrote J a letter and told him that despite what we had done that I was still going to marry you. I never heard from him after that. I bumped into a friend of his in town a while back; that's when I found out about the accident."

Theo looked up at the sky; a new day had fully arrived. "You say you didn't think of me as a fool. But you right when you said I wouldn't have married you. I'm standin' here lookin' at you, and after all des years of sleepin' in the same bed wid you, I don't know who you are. So all this anger you have toward Lindie is cause if she hadn't come along, you could 'a married another man . . . the man you really loved? Am I right, Ruby?"

"I grew to love you, Theo."

"That ain't what I asked you! I loved you when we got married, and now it all makes sense, all des years you've had so much bitterness in yo' heart, there ain't been too much room left for love. After hearin' all this, it don't really matter to me right now if you don't love me, but . . . that girl . . . it ain't her fault what her momma did befo' she got married. You ought to at least have yo' head straight on that by now. Guess I held onto a one-sided love too long. Move away from the car!"

"What're you going to do?" Ruby yelled at her husband as she watched him get back in the car. He revved the engine and backed up to the paved road.

"I don't know what I'm goin' to do, and you can think 'bout what you goin' do while you walk back to the house. One thing fo' sure, Ruby, you was blessed wid a good set of lyin' eyes!" After shouting out his response, Theo screeched away like a drag racer.

Ruby fell to her knees with her hands raised to the sky, "Please forgive me Lord . . . please forgive me." Her tears fell in buckets for several minutes because one penalty for deceit is profound hurt. The distant horn of a tugboat coming up the river prompted her to pull herself together. She stood up and started to walk back home knowing that her relationship with her husband had taken a blow from which it might not recover. She wiped away tears as rapidly as they fell.

3

Theo had been driving in a daze, unaware of the miles he had clocked or the time that had passed. He was also hungry and thirsty. When he glanced at the gas gauge, he realized he was nearly driving on fumes. Although still on the Shore, he was a good distance from Fullerton when he pulled into a graveled lot in front of an aged wooden structure that was passing as a filling station/store. The exterior of the structure was plastered with dated posters that had been faded by the sun or harsh winter weather, making Conway Twitty and George Jones barely recognizable. He walked into the store and saw the store keeper (a tall slender white man) bent over the counter reading a newspaper. No one else was around. A honky-tonk ditty was playing on a dusty brown radio positioned on a shelf behind the store keeper. A fan decorated with cob webs adorned the ceiling above the counter. Theo extended a greeting, but the store keeper did not respond. Nonetheless, a thirsty and hungry Theo slapped $2.25 down on the counter and said, "Two dollars' worth of gasoline and a cold ginger ale."

The store keeper retrieved a cigar box from under the counter and shoved the money into it. Without even looking at Theo, he removed a ginger ale from the cooler and slid it down the counter toward his customer. He then pointed to a bottle opener on the opposite end of the cooler. This caught Theo off guard because he had expected the soda to be handed to him. He let that insult pass. Once Theo saw how dirty the store keeper's hands were, he decided against asking for a few slices of bologna and walked out of the store.

After pumping his own gasoline, Theo felt the need to relieve himself. As he approached the bathroom door with a rusty door knob on the outside of the store, the store keeper shouted out, "Hey! You can't use that bathroom."

Theo looked up and above the door of the bathroom was a handwritten sign, *whites only.*

"Where's the colored bathroom?"

"Ain't one . . . you gotta go in the woods behind the store."

"Come on man! I just bought gas and a soda here, and you won't let me use this rundown bathroom? I'll be gone fo' 'nother customer shows up."

"You heared what I said; ain't no bathroom for you, boy. There's a outhouse in the woods that coloreds use."

Theo had to temper his anger; after all, there was a Virginia license plate on the pickup parked next to the store. He assumed the pickup belonged to the store keeper. Most people on the lower shore of Maryland knew that the eastern Shore of Virginia was decidedly immune to progress on many levels.

Even though the bathroom insult burned, Theo began to make his way through the brush that had sprouted up early for April perhaps due to the recent rainy weather. Had it not been for the fact that his bladder was full, he told himself he would have skidded away from the gas stop leaving a flurry of gravel behind. However, with the drive from Dearmount and his sudden departure from home, he had been driving for so long, he needed to empty his bladder.

That pimple-faced cracker ought to be glad I don't live near here, cause I'm a mind to snatch down that "whites only" sign and set fire to the place. Ain't like my piss is any worse than a white man's; they don't need no special bathroom." A few steps more is when Theo saw the outhouse just beyond a murky stream of water swirling with twigs and leaves, but an occupant was already there. A black snake was slithering through an opening at the bottom of the door. Theo picked up a heavy branch from the ground and began a lethal attack on the reptile. By the time he had worked off the frustration with his wife and the gas stop attendant, the snake was no more than a bloody, wacked up mass. In the process of hacking away at the snake, Theo wet his pants. He trotted (shaking one leg then another) back to his car and drove away.

4

It had taken Ruby about 45 minutes to walk home from the ferry crossing. At least two passersby recognized her and stopped to ask if she needed a ride. She refused both and used the time during her walk to contemplate the tangled mess she was now involved in. Indeed it was wrong to have married Theo without telling him she was expecting a baby by another man, but she was also guilty of holding a grudge against Lindie even before she was born. Now that her husband knew the truth, she would have to find a way to make amends with him. Doing so would likely mean she would have to humble herself like never before. She wasn't sure she had the skills necessary to undertake such a personal transformation or if she even knew where to begin. She would need help to rectify a dastardly deed she had committed to cover up a lapse in judgement that occurred in the heat of an ill-fated romance.

Ruby walked into the house and found it as quiet as an empty church. She eased open the door to the bedroom shared by her youngest two, and they were sound asleep. She looked toward Lindie's door but decided not to open it. Instead, she went into the living room and rested for a while before placing the first of two important telephone calls. The party line was clear when she picked up the receiver. If she really wanted to get her life back on a normal track, the first call could not be delayed.

He picked up on the second ring, "Hello."

"It's me," she whispered. "Just listen to what I have to say cause I can't talk long. You can't come around here anymore, and I won't be meeting you anywhere ever again."

He scrambled to get a few words in, but Ruby cut him off, "I'm not kidding. I've got a big problem here at home. If you see me in town or anywhere for that matter, just pretend you don't know who I am, because I won't recognize you. Something's happened at home that I can't talk about, and I can't fix it if I'm involved with you. I've got to hang up before somebody picks up on this line, goodbye." She placed the receiver back on the cradle, slumped into a chair, and started to weep quietly. With that call she hoped she had ended what had not yet become a full-fledged affair with a man that unbeknownst to her, Lindie had seen her kissing.

The telephone rang, but Ruby, assuming it was the man she had just spoken with, picked up the receiver and slammed it back down. After she stemmed the flow of tears, she placed another call. Four rings and finally someone on the other end picked up. Thankfully it was the person she wanted to speak with.

"Fred."

He immediately picked up on his sister's distressed tone. "What's wrong? Ya'll still coming?"

"We . . . we had to come back home."

"Back home? Barbara had everything set up for ya'll to spend the day."

"There was an awful scene at Aunt Nita's, and now Theo's upset with me. He's not here now, and I don't know where he went or if he's coming back."

"What the hell . . . what awful scene?"

"I can't talk about it on the phone."

"Theo ain't never seemed like the kind of man to run off and leave his family. What's he upset about?"

"I just told you I can't talk about it on the phone. You know we have a party line. I just wanted to know if he had called you."

"He ain't called here, and soon as I take a shower, I'm headed down there."

"If you insist, but come by yourself."

"I will, and you need to pull yourself together before the girls see you all upset."

After the call ended, Ruby moved to the couch and tossed her head back on a cushion. While staring at the ceiling, all kinds of thoughts raced through her head. That's when she heard a soft tapping at the front door. She peeped through the curtain and saw her nuisance brother-in-law.

Oh my God. I forgot all about him. She reluctantly opened the door. "What do you want, Marvin?"

She smelled the alcohol before he even opened his mouth, "Where's Theo? You twooo left here in the carrr, but I ain't see him drop youuu off. You walked up tooo the house. He's supposed to take me to catch the busss back to Baltimore."

"I can use the pickup to take you in town, or better yet, my brother will be here in a couple of hours. Go on back to the tavern, and don't put your grimy paws on another bottle of our whiskey."

"I need tooo use the bathroom."

"You could 'a used the one in the tavern."

"Got tooo go real bad."

Go head."

Ruby remained at the front door until Marvin finished and later ushered him out the door as though he were a leper. "Remember what I said about our whiskey."

When Ruby flopped back down on the couch again, she started to remember how often, over the years, she had told herself that the truth would surely come out one day. However, after she heard about J's death, she stopped fearing the when and how, believing that her secret would remain a secret forever. On the day she married Theo, her father had offered a piece of advice. He said, "Ruby, life can kick you in the gut sometimes, but I think Theo's a good man who will stand by you through thick and thin, so you've got to be a good wife. Sometimes the best gifts don't come wrapped up all neat in fancy packages," It was that last line of her father's that had stayed with her through the years. There was nothing fancy about her husband and his broken English.

Well, Daddy, life had already kicked me in the gut, but I couldn't tell you that. Umm, maybe it's from me that Lindie inherited the ability to keep secrets so well. If those letters had burned up before she found them, I sure wouldn't be going through this.

Ruby was jolted back to real time when she heard Lindie calling from her bedroom, "Daddy, I'm hungry."

Ruby jumped up quickly because she did not want Lindie to awaken her sisters. She paused just long enough to holster her anger at Lindie before she opened her daughter's bedroom door. "He's not here, and your sisters are asleep, so keep your voice down."

"But I'm hungry."

Ruby looked at the food Lindie hadn't touched. "You need to eat what your sister brought you earlier."

"Where's Daddy?"

"I'm not in the mood for answering questions, especially from you right now."

"Can I have my journal?"

Ruby had to catch herself before she snapped. After all, she was staring at the person she believed to be at the root of her current problem. "I don't know where it is. Your daddy. . . Theo put it some place."

Ruby didn't give Lindie a chance to respond before she closed the door and went into the kitchen. She pulled out ingredients to make Maryland beaten biscuits. She would likely awaken Francine and Vinnie, but she needed to occupy herself with something productive. Plus, she hoped that all the pounding required for making such biscuits would help her release some frustration. Biscuits would be ready by the time her brother arrived. Once all the ingredients were in a large bowl, she turned the radio on and fidgeted with the tuning knob until she was able to pull in an AM station without too much static. The disc jockey was spinning Dean Martin's version of *Red Roses for a Blue Lady.* Not exactly the best song for her to listen to given her state of mind at the time, but it was better than listening to the bluegrass jamborees that drifted from the other static-free radio stations.

5

About fifteen miles outside of Fullerton, Theo had a change of heart. He was not ready to go back home and face his wife again. He needed more time to mull over the gut-wrenching news she had delivered, causing him to descend into a state of uncertainty about his marriage. He drove to another village where a first cousin, Ben lived. Theo had not bothered too much with Ben over the last couple of years, because Helen (Ben's third wife—a biracial woman) was a bit much to take with her highfalutin, big city ways. She used to write a column on style and social events for a colored newspaper in Washington, DC. Since she considered herself to have been an important newspaper columnist, she insisted that everything around her be just so, and that was something a country boy like Theo was not used to. He was no stranger to roughing it. Plus, Helen had a way of pointing her fingers with long dark red nails and flicking her salt and pepper hair around like white women. Theo and his family had little to do with them. There was even a time when Ruby told Theo she thought Helen was a stuck-up witch who looked down her nose at them.

Stuck-up or not, Theo was desperate to find solace somewhere, and he hoped that his cousin's home would be a temporary safe haven. Theo and Ben had been close as children, and Ben served as Theo's best man at his wedding. Theo would lean on that back-in-the-day familiarity at a time when he truly needed another man's perspective on his current dilemma.

Roughly thirty minutes later, after pondering his decision over and over about dropping in without an invitation and allowing time for his wet pants to dry, he pulled up behind one of the two gleaming Fords parked on Ben's driveway. It was Helen who met him at the door. "Well bless my heart, look who's come for a visit."

"Mornin', Helen. You lookin' well, so that means Ben's takin' good care of you."

"Yes indeed he is . . . Ben . . . get yourself down here . . . we have company, and he looks a little worse for the wear."

"I didn't get no sleep last night, so . . . ."

At the base of the steps, Ben cut Theo's sentence off, "Theo Mitchell, we ain't seen you in a month of Sundays . . . matter of fact, longer than that. What brings you here? Don't tell me somebody died."

Theo glanced at Helen and was reluctant to offer his cousin an honest answer in front of her. "Nah . . . that ain't why I stopped by. Wonder if me and you could chew the fat man-to-man?"

"Oh, I'm not supposed to hear this men's conversation? That's okay, but I bet if I fix us a nice meal, you'll stay for a bit and we can all talk then?"

Theo looked at Ben for approval. "If it's okay wid you?"

"Then it's settled. While Helen stirs up a meal, you and me can go sit under the tree and talk because something must really be wrong."

"You like Waldorf salad, Theo, and sparkling wine?" asked Helen.

"I ain't never heard of Waldorf salad and ain't never had no sparklin' wine."

"That's okay. I like introducing country folks to different things."

"She don't mean no harm, Theo. Remember, she grew up in New York City."

Theo and Ben settled into a couple of chairs under a tree, and within minutes, the dejected husband was extracting a pledge of silence from his cousin before he started spilling his story.

"When we was growin' up, we was almost like brothers, you and me. You ever hear anybody call me a fool behind my back?"

"Not that I recall right off the bat."

"What I got to say is real serious."

"How come you're confiding in me . . . we ain't been close in a spell?"

"Ain't like you's a total stranger. Marvin's at the house, but he ain't got no head for what I'm dealin' wid. Ain't no way to say it but straight out." Theo fought back tears and continued, "I found out early this mornin' that my oldest daughter . . . Lindie . . . well, she ain't really my child."

Ben was stunned, "The hell you say? The one that was always writing in a book as I remember?"

Theo nodded a confirmation. "Still writin' in a book . . . Ruby just told me after all des years."

"Did you and Ruby have a fight, and maybe she just said this to hurt you?"

"No. It weren't like that."

Over the course of the next 45 minutes, Theo shared everything, starting with how troublesome the relationship between Ruby and Lindie had been for some time.

"Would you go back to a woman that did somethin' like this to you?"

Ben stood up and walked around, thinking and simultaneously rubbing the back of his neck with one hand. He'd had tons of experience with women and was now married to his third wife.

"Man, I don't know what I'd do. What about the other two girls? They yours?"

"They mine unless she was tippin' out after we got married."

"If I was you, I'd ask Ruby for sure. Either way, if you leave your family where would you go? And you know how bad people would talk about you—just another trifling colored man who up and left his family."

"I'm the only Daddy dem girls know."

"Do you love Ruby enough to stay?"

"I don't know. I been ridin' 'round wid thoughts all up in my head like a crazy man since early this mornin', and I don't know how to answer that question. I guess a person don't stop carin' 'bout somebody all of a sudden like."

"I didn't ask if you still cared about Ruby; you can care about a person and not love them. You need to decide if you love your wife enough to stay. You go to church much?"

"Now and then. I go more than she does."

"Maybe talk it over with your pastor."

Theo released a long sigh, threw his head back, closed his eyes, and shook his head from side to side. "I been such a fool, and I should 'a knowed somethin' wasn't right. Should 'a kept my behind in school; then I'd a had more common sense like you."

"Common sense ain't taught in school; it comes from living. How about this . . . if you don't want to go home right now . . . stay here with us for the rest of the day, even the night and then go back and face Ruby. Sure as the cock crows, you got to do it sooner or later. It ain't gonna get no easier if you drag your feet about it. You can't keep driving around all day wasting gas while trying to get your head together."

"You don't think Helen will mind if I spend the night? I ain't got no change of clothes or nothin' wid me fo' spendin' the night."

"If you know Helen, you know she likes to have company over, and she makes sure I always got plenty clean clothes. There's a convenience store open up the road a bit. We can at least get you a toothbrush, and I'll give you a new pair of boxers right out of the bag from Sears and Roebuck."

Helen interrupted Theo's true confession. "You all ready to eat? I fixed a Waldorf Salad, tuna melts, and cream of tomato soup."

"We coming, and Theo's going to spend the night."

"Wonderful. The guest room is already set up, and there's a robe and bedroom slippers in the closet."

Ben patted his cousin on the back as they walked back to the house. "You'll figure out what you got to do."

"Can we go up to that store befo' we eat? I can't sit at Helen's table dirty like I am?"

"Sure thing. Let me grab my keys and tell Helen we'll be right back."

6

Meanwhile, back at the Mitchell house Vinnie walked into the kitchen just as her mother was removing the beaten biscuits from the oven.

"Momma, are you fixing something else to eat? All we had was toast and juice."

"Is Francine up too?"

"No, she's pretending to be sleep. How come Lindie can't talk to us?"

"One thing at a time. You want breakfast or lunch?"

"Breakfast . . . sausage, pancakes, and applesauce."

"Don't worry about Lindie, she'll be coming out later."

Before Vinnie could respond, a car pulled into the driveway, so of course she ran to see who it was. "Momma, it's Uncle Fred!"

Ruby joined her youngest at the door. "Go grab a comic book or turn the TV on; I have some business to discuss with your uncle. When Ruby opened the door to let her brother in, she welcomed his embrace, but with Vinnie nearby, she couldn't reveal what was wrong.

"I'm glad you came alone."

"So tell me what's going on."

"We can talk in the kitchen."

Once in the kitchen, Fred didn't waste any time getting to the purpose of his hasty trip to the shore. "Tell me why you think my brother-in-law has run off."

Ruby motioned for her brother to take a seat at the table before she began to share the deeply personal secret that was now gnawing at her gut. "In the wee hours of this morning while we were still at Aunt Nita's, I was awakened by a lot of shouting downstairs. I reached for Theo and realized he wasn't in the bed, so I ran downstairs, and there he was with Alvin and Lindie. She had attempted to run away, and Theo caught her."

"Ahh, come on, Ruby."

"It's true. Theo had been out on Aunt Nita's back porch smoking when Lindie tipped through the back door carrying a paper sack with some of her personal belongings in it. He demanded that she go back in the house, and that's when all the shouting started. Alvin beat me downstairs. When Theo explained what had happened, I laid into your niece and told her how she was embarrassing the family. I tried to knock the color off her and ordered her back to bed. But once again, she turned on me, and by then everybody was up."

"I guess this gets worse since ya'll came back home."

"She decided to pay me back by blurting out something about me marrying a man I didn't love just because I was pregnant." Ruby began to cry again.

"Say what?"

"That's what she implied."

"Something she made up?"

Ruby braced herself and continued, "No . . . She had found some old love letters I used to keep in the back of my bedroom closet in the old house. I didn't know she had found them."

"Woo, woo . . . wait a minute. You mean it's true . . . you were pregnant when you and Theo got married? Why would that cause him to be so upset now?"

Ruby leaned back in her chair and stared at her brother as more tears dripped down her face. Now she had to share with her brother what she considered the worst part of the drama, "Because it was another man's child."

Fred's eyes lit up as he shot up from his chair as though it were on fire. He looked at his sister in total disbelief. "Oh Jesus Lawd . . . So you went to one of those women who handle that kind of problem?"

"No. I was scared something would go wrong, and it was too close to my wedding date."

"I'm missing something here. How'd you get rid of the baby?"

Ruby lowered her head before she responded, "I didn't get rid of the baby."

"The hell you saying woman?" Then he thought for a second. "Hold on a sec . . . Lindie is Theo's child, right?"

Ruby shook her head in response as her brother's body language indicated profound disgust. "Before you judge me so harshly let me finish . . . I couldn't have told Daddy; he would have thrown me out of the house, and Momma would have been so ashamed of me. My wedding to Theo had already been announced," Ruby started to cry again.

"Oh my God . . . ain't this a fine mess . . . so who's Lindie's father?"

"It doesn't matter now cause he's dead."

Through gritted teeth Fred demanded, "I don't care, I still want to know who it was. I drove down here in a rush to be by your side with no idea how serious the problem was. You got to tell me everything."

Ruby rose from her chair, walked over to the kitchen door and kept her back to her brother as she explained, "His name was Louis, but he went by J."

"And where the hell did you meet him? There was nobody named Louis in Fullerton when we were growing up."

"None of that matters now, Fred. It was many years ago."

"I can't believe this. I grew up in the same house with you, and we rarely left Fullerton. Did you and your secret lover sneak into the woods when nobody else was around?"

Ruby protested with much indignation, "I never sneaked into the woods with anybody."

"Too late to be acting all high and mighty, sis, so where'd you meet him?"

"In Brookville and then we met there a few times before he went off to college. After he was settled in college we starting exchanging letters. Somehow he heard I was getting married, and he came home one weekend and surprised me."

"And left you with a gift." Fred was nearly in a state of shock. "You know, I do remember some letters you used to get for a spell--always had a Virginia postmark. You said you had a girlfriend that you met on a Sunday school trip. So that was a lie. Now Theo knows the truth. Let me guess . . . he feels like the biggest fool ever. So would I if I were in his shoes."

Ruby fell silent while her brother took it all in.

"Lawd, Lawd, Lawd. When you called, I thought ya'll had a fight over something related to the tavern. I never could have guessed this."

"What if he doesn't come back?"

"I don't know, sis. This'd be hard for any man to get his head around. It's bad enough you tricked him, but to find out the way he did. This stings."

"I didn't trick him."

"What do you call it, Ruby? You married him when you knew you were expecting a baby by another man, and you let him believe he's the girl's father all this time. That took a lot of nerve."

"I wanted your support, not for you to come down here and treat me like some evil person. So you can just get in your car and head back to Philly."

"Just calm down. You brought this on yourself."

Ruby didn't have a rebuttal.

"All these years Barbara and I have wondered why you've been so hard on Lindie. Now I know--she's been a reminder of what you did, and you've held it against her. Jesus Christ, Ruby. I'm your only sibling, and I love you, but I'm a tell you the God honest truth whether you want to hear it or not. You been wrong to hold it against that girl and now you're paying for it. She didn't choose you as her mother, but you chose to bring her into this world. You're the adult; you didn't have your stuff together back then, but you need to get it together now and in a hurry."

"I told her she was going to be sent to reform school for showing off in front of company and embarrassing the family like she did. Second time she's embarrassed me in front of people."

"You don't even realize how crazy you sound—punishing her for your sin. When this gets out, Lindie ain't going to be the one people be pointing fingers at. Like hell she's going to a reform school. Before that happens, she'll come to Philly and live with me and my family."

For the next few minutes brother and sister sat in silence. Ruby was on the verge of complete emotional exhaustion. Fred threw an occasional glance at his sister and wondered how she could have kept such a secret for so long. Ruby was once again going over the details from earlier that morning followed by the talk she had with her husband. Guilt was weighing heavily upon her when she broke the silence and asked her brother again, "What if he doesn't come back?"

"Theo's got a good heart. He's the only father Lindie has known, and he has two . . ." Fred paused and stared at his sister. She sensed what he was thinking.

"Of course they're his kids."

"Okay then, he has two other kids. I don't think he'll abandon them. He's off somewhere licking his wounds."

"I have a wound too."

"Yeah, but you've had a long time to deal with yours, and it was self-inflicted. Theo's wound is fresh and you did it."

Fred rose to leave the kitchen.

"Where're you going?"

"To find my niece and to tell her she ain't going to be sent off to no damn reform school . . . unless you want to tell her."

Ruby waved her brother on just before he knocked on Lindie's door.

"Lindie . . . you dressed? It's Uncle Fred."

Lindie hopped out of her bed and opened her door with a half-smile on her face. "What're you doing here, Uncle Fred?"

Fred flashed a wide imposter's grin. "Surprise, surprise! I thought maybe you were in here writing in that little book of yours."

"They hid it someplace."

"You can go play with your sisters, and you ain't being shipped off to reform school. I'll try to find out what happened to your book before I leave."

"Momma told you what I did?"

"We not going to talk about that now; go on and find your sisters."

"Where's Aunt Barbara and the kids?"

"They all home in Philly. Your momma's gonna talk to you later."

The smile quickly disappeared from Lindie's face. "Does that mean she's not going to beat me?"

"No she's not."

Lindie waited until her uncle walked away before she entered her sisters' bedroom where she found Francine with crayons and a coloring book. Vinnie joined them. While Lindie was able to breathe a huge sigh of relief about not being sent to reform school, she wondered what other punishment she would receive after her uncle left. She had done a very bad thing by trying to run away, and she could not imagine that her mother would be in a forgiving mood, given the dramatic scene that had played out in Dearmount.

Fred returned to the kitchen and watched as his sister placed some rope sausage in a skillet. Cooking was therapeutic for Ruby.

"There's some biscuits wrapped in the dish towel."

"I told her you weren't gonna beat her and that she ain't going to reform school. She looked like she didn't believe me, but she's in with her sisters now. You got any idea where Theo might have gone?"

"No."

Fred looked at his watch. "I'm a hang around for a few hours and hope he shows up, but I gotta be to work early tomorrow morning . . . even if Theo don't come back, you got to make a decision about whether you're gonna tell Lindie about her real daddy."

Ruby abruptly turned to face her brother and stated firmly, "Theo's the only father she's known, and I'm fine leaving it that way."

"What if Theo feels differently? It can't just be what you want; that kind of thinking help get you into this fix."

"For your information, I didn't want to get pregnant."

"That ain't what I meant. You needed a husband before your belly showed everybody what you had been doing. What's done in the dark is revealed in the light, so you decided to use Theo instead of telling Daddy you didn't want to marry him."

"Listen to you being so righteous. What if it had been you and your girlfriend?"

"No way. Daddy talked to me over and over about wearing a hat to the party, and I ain't being righteous. I'm just saying out loud what anybody who knew the truth would be thinking. You know I'm right. Daddy sure would 'a punished you . . . but J, he might have hunted him down like a dog. Poor Momma would have been humiliated in front of her friends after all that preaching she did about keeping your dress down and your legs closed when we was teenagers. I remember how she used to talk to you."

"Okay Fred. That was a long time ago. In the heat of the moment I wasn't thinking about what Momma said." Ruby needed to change the subject, "You going to eat with me and the girls or not?"

Without waiting for her brother's response, Ruby starting making pancakes. She didn't admit it to her brother (who was flipping through the pages of a newspaper) but rolling around and around in her head were thoughts of what the encounter with her husband would be if he ever returned. Dealing with Lindie would have to come later as she prioritized the things she needed to do. First she would serve a late breakfast, followed by a shower and change of clothes. She had done her hair a couple of days ago, but she would add a few curls and waves plus put on the dress Theo liked best on her—all in anticipation of his return. Then she would send the girls outside to play while, in solitude, she would await her husband's return, hoping he would be in a frame of mind to discuss rather than argue.

With the sausage and pancakes ready, she asked Fred to get his nieces to the table.

"Is Daddy outside?" asked Vinnie.

"Your daddy went to visit someone," stated Fred in a deadpan manner, while avoiding eye contact with his niece. Lindie saw the quick glances that darted back and forth between her mother and uncle, so she sensed they were hiding something.

"Ya'll eat your breakfast and then clean up the dishes. Later you can go outside and play. Don't get any dirt in your hair cause tomorrow's a school day."

Ruby could feel Lindie's eyes fixed on her, watching for any sign of a crack in her façade, so she avoided looking directly at her. That would come soon enough, and Ruby suspected it would be more like two adults talking instead of mother and child. How Lindie had gotten to be so grown up for her age she didn't know. But she knew for sure she didn't want another blow-up to occur before she had a chance to deal with the man who abandoned her at the ferry crossing and made her walk home while he took off for parts unknown.

After the meal, Fred announced he would busy himself with the activity he normally undertook when he visited his sister and her family in the spring and summer months. He retrieved a sickle from the shed and proceeded to whack down weeds wherever he found them. The girls finished the dishes as ordered and went outside to play—Lindie included. They prepared mud pies while Ruby prepped for her husband's possible return.

Around 4 p.m., Fred informed his sister that he needed to head back to Philly and asked her to call him as soon as she heard from her husband. He also suggested that whoever had hidden Lindie's journal should return it.

"After all, writing in a book is way more innocent than a lot of things I can think of. I will have to share all of this with Barbara. It was all I could do to keep her from hopping in the car with me to come down here."

After Fred summoned Marvin from the tavern, he released the brake on his car and began to back away, but he had one last thing to say to his sister who was standing near his car. He didn't mind sharing what he had to say in front of Marvin who, despite Ruby's warning, had managed to get himself liquored up on cheap whiskey from the tavern. He wouldn't accurately process anything he overheard. "Ruby, once things are broken, they can't be unbroken. Trust has been broken here, and the truth ain't gonna die. Maybe you and Theo will need some help—like talking to your pastor."

Marvin had settled himself on the back seat of Fred's car and started singing a slurred line from Brook Benton's "Rainy Night in Georgia." That was Fred's clue to get him (although drunk) to the bus depot as fast as possible, and Ruby was left to think about her brother's parting words.

Broken, so what will I do? She went to her bedroom and stretched out on her bed hoping to rest, but rest evaded her. She picked up a book of poems that had survived the fire that destroyed their home the year before. She then gathered all three of her daughters and read several poems, starting with *I Had but Fifty Cents,* author unknown. Francine and Vinnie appreciated the humor in the first poem. An outsider looking on would have seen their smiling faces and believed everything to be fine with the Mitchells. So many truths lie dormant behind smiles.

"Why you dressed up Momma; you going somewhere?" asked Vinnie.

"Nope—not going anywhere."

"Where's Daddy been all day?" asked Francine.

Ruby and Lindie's eyes met before Ruby responded, "He had something to attend to, and right now ya'll need to play together or something till bedtime. I got some chores to do."

By 8:30 p.m. the girls were asleep. There was no sign of Theo and no call. Ruby sat on the couch with her eyes glued to a front window waiting and watching—waiting and watching. When the kitchen clock struck midnight, she crawled into bed fully dressed and wept with only the darkness to embrace her.

7

Theo had declined Helen's offer for a nightcap. He also told Ben he wasn't up to a game of checkers. Instead, he retreated to the guest room, and there, for the first time since his wife had delivered her astounding news, he allowed feelings of self-pity and insecurity to alter his state of mind like never before. He was on his knees and completely unstrung.

How could I have been such a idiot? I was head-over-heels wid that woman. She had my nose wide open, and I didn't even sense that maybe she didn't feel the same way 'bout me. I thought she was a timid bride who'd have to warm up to performin' wifely duties. Now that I think back on it, her father seemed more anxious that we get married than she did, and I was too stupid to see it. What am I gonna do now? After all des years I find out my oldest daughter ain't really my child. I always knowed somethin' was different 'bout her, but I just thought she took after Ruby more than me, and damn straight she do, cause ain't none of me in her. Lawd . . . you gotta help me figure this out.

Theo began to undress and angrily threw his clothes onto the floor. After he donned the robe and slippers offered by Helen, he went to the bathroom and took a long shower. The flow of the shower disguised the tears he let fall as he braced himself against the wall. No shower would ever be able to wash away the hurt, the humiliation, and the ultimate feeling of betrayal he felt. *If my neighbors and other family members find out, I can just see their faces now—pitying the fool.*

As he lay in bed waiting for sleep to silence his misery, he even questioned if he was a real man. *A man ain't nothin' if he ain't got no pride.* He told himself a real man would have uncovered the truth long before he had. Truth be told, if it had not been for Lindie, he may have never found out. The truth would have remained hidden far from his reality. *I will be forever grateful to her, despite how it came to light, but can I ever forgive my wife? Should I?* As the cuckoo clock in the living room signaled midnight, the curtain closed on the horrors that had defined the day, and allowed a troubled man to fall asleep.

Back at the Mitchell house, Ruby had fallen asleep. Lindie had gotten out of bed to go to the bathroom, but she also looked out a window for Theo's car. It was not there. Then she listened at her parent's bedroom door. Only silence. While she didn't know the details, she assumed something was seriously wrong. She could not remember a time when her father had stayed away all night.

8

At 5 a.m. the next morning, a startled Ruby made a dash from her bed to the ringing telephone in the living room. But her hopes were crushed when she heard the voice on the other end.

"Ruby, what'd ya'll mean putting Marvin on a bus while he was all liquored up? Plus he got back to Baltimore in the wee hours of the morning. It was 4 a.m. when he called me from the bus station slurring his words. It's a wonder somebody didn't knock him in the head and take his wallet."

Ruby took a deep breath before she responded to her sister-in-law in a slow and low but firm tone, "Christine, I'm going to say this just one time. Don't ever call here again ranting and raving about Marvin. Your wino brother is your responsibility and the least of my concerns. You should 'a never sent him down here to begin with."

"Put my brother on the phone! I don't have to take this kind 'a talk from you."

Ruby slammed the receiver back onto the cradle. After she abruptly ended the call, she thought about leaving the receiver off the hook, but quick thinking reminded her that Theo might call. She then realized she was still wearing clothes from the day before. She changed into her robe and lay back down for another hour or so before getting the girls up for school. She hadn't set out their clothes; nor had she packed their lunches. It would be a hectic morning. *If that woman calls me right back, I swear I'm gonna lose my mind.* Christine and Marvin's issues were never on Ruby's agenda. She often teetered on the verge of loathing both of them. Truth be told, both had been sources of contention between Ruby and Theo for all the years of their marriage—one a drunk and the other a fat, bossy spinster.

Once lunch pails were packed for school, Ruby set up the ironing board to press clothes for each of her daughters. By the time she was done, it was time for the girls to get dressed and to eat breakfast. Ruby anticipated that Lindie would be the one to ask where Theo was, but she was wrong.

As she fidgeted with the scrapple and toast on her plate, Francine asked, "Where's Daddy?"

Under the circumstances, the last thing Ruby wanted to do was to be caught in a lie. "He left to visit someone yesterday and he's not back yet. Don't start a string of questions. You have a bus to catch. Finish eating and get dressed."

Lindie was deliberately silent. She kept her eyes glued to her plate until she finished her breakfast rather than looking at her mother. Unbeknownst to Ruby, guilt was also weighing on Lindie's mind. Was she the reason her father hadn't come home last night? Was he ever coming back? This particular situation was not something she wanted to record in her journal, nor could she talk to anyone about how she was feeling. How would someone her age know what words to use to describe the current situation—brought on by her? A lesson she learned in the aftermath of her failed attempt to escape, was that a person can't always blurt out words that have the potential to harm, no matter how angry a person might become. The consequences could be harsher than the words. What Lindie could not have known then was the dysfunction that defined her family then would likely continue to define them for the rest of their lives.

9

Theo was awakened by loud knocks on the guestroom door. As Ben peeped inside the room where Theo was sleeping, he inquired, "Hey man, you good? It's almost 8 o'clock. You going to have breakfast here?"

"No, man . . . 8 o'clock? I'm a throw on my clothes and get goin'."

"You going home?"

As he sat upright in the bed, he looked Ben square in the eyes. "I reckon I got to sooner or later. Can't keep droppin' in on relatives."

"And then?"

"We see 'bout then when then git here."

With that said, Ben closed the door allowing his cousin to dress in private. It didn't take Theo but a couple of minutes to throw on his clothes and shoes.

"I really 'preciate you lettin' me stay here last night, but I got to go now. Tell yo' wife thanks for everythin'. I won't stay a stranger so long this time."

"Take it easy now, and maybe think about talking with your pastor."

Theo acknowledged Ben's response with a look that meant he doubted that would happen, and then he was gone—out to his car heading for Fullerton. While he was dressing, he had decided he would ask Ruby what she wanted to do and to see if it jived with what he had determined was the only option. But as he approached the outskirts of Fullerton, he changed his mind. He would not ask Ruby what she wanted to do. Instead, he would take control of the situation and not leave it up to somebody who had already fooled him in the worst way. He would lay out his decision. *She can leave if she wants to, but dem girls will stay wid me. I wouldn't care 'bout what folks might say, and if she didn't already tell Lindie 'bout that other man, she'll never be told 'bout him, cause I'm her real Daddy.*

Ruby heard a car on the driveway, and when she peeped through the living room drapes, she felt a degree of relief. However, too much remained unsettled for her to take too much joy in the return of her husband. *Was he back to stay or to say goodbye for good?*

Theo knew the girls would be off to school by then. He entered the house with a veil of false bravado in place and stood just inside the kitchen door. "Ruby . . . where you at?"

Ruby entered the kitchen, smoothing out the front of her

dress and patting down her hair to tame any wayward strands. "I'm glad you decided to come back. When you left me at the ferry I . . . I wasn't sure you'd come back."

"I need you to listen to what I got to say, and hear me good cause I'm a cut to the chase. Have you told Lindie that yo' old flame is her real daddy?"

"Of course not. As far as I'm concerned, you are her father."

"You say this other man's dead. So unless you been mixed up in some other dirty deeds, Francine and Vinnie are my kids, and I'm not gonna let a bad decision you made years ago take my kids away from me now. . . . you and me—that's 'nother story. Dem girls, they the best part of my life—the reason I get up early and haul junk from place to place, the reason why I work for that white dentist, and the reason why I sell beer and cheap wine even though some people along this road thumb they noses at me for runnin' a tavern. But like I said, you and me . . . I don't know. I ain't gonna make you leave. You'll never be able to say to dem girls that their daddy threw their momma out, but if you want to, I ain't gonna get in yo' way. If you stay, don't be lookin' fo' me to slide over to yo' side of the bed anytime soon, sista."

"I know it's going to take a while for you to forgive me, and I don't think we should ever tell Lindie the truth?"

"I ain't said nothin' 'bout forgivin'. I said I wasn't gonna make you leave, and no, we ain't tellin' Lindie nothin'. If you change yo' mind and go behind my back and tell her, you got to pack yo' bags—no ifs, ands, or buts 'bout it. I'm her daddy—always have been . . . always will be. And you're gonna ease up on her startin' today. When dem girls come home today, or when anybody comes 'round, you got to act like we okay. When people see me, I'll be like the song say, *My Smile is Just a Frown turned upside down.*"

"So I'm supposed to stay in a loveless marriage?"

"You ain't got to stay—yo' choice. I got a haulin' job to get done." Theo turned to leave.

"But, Theo . . . ."

"I'm done talkin' for now. Rustle up some cornbread and smothered pork chops for dinner.

O-u-r children loves pork chops."

"Aren't you going to tell me where you were last night?"

"Said I'm done talkin' for now."

As Ruby watched her husband head towards his pickup, mixed feelings bounced around in her head about whether they would be able to patch things up. She was relieved he had returned, but she feared the person she was watching had changed overnight. How could she live without physical intimacy? She had recently terminated the beginnings of a fling, and now nothing--even though her fire had not burned out. Was this the penance she would have to pay for her misdeed from years ago? *Momma used to say, 'Oh what a tangled web we weave when first we practice to deceive.' She said that to me more than once, and she didn't even know about my secret. She didn't hear me on the early mornings when I was throwing up in the bathroom. At least I don't think she did, but she died before Lindie was born. She didn't get a chance to say, 'She don't look nothing like Theo'---That's right, she looks just like me, and that helped me keep the truth hidden all this time.*

At the dinner table that evening, the frostiness between the parents went completely unnoticed by their youngest two daughters—not so with Lindie. "Where were you last night, Daddy?"

Theo was ready with a quick answer and half smile because he expected Lindie to be the one to inquire about his overnight absence. "I had to see Cousin Ben and his wife. Cousin Helen whipped up one of her fancy meals . . . 'member she's from New York City, and they invited me to spend the night." Doing what he could to diffuse Lindie's possible speculations, Theo continued. "Cousin Helen even put out a nice, fluffy robe and some house shoes for me to use after I took a long hot shower. They treated me like a king, and I slept like a baby."

"A robe and slippers offered to a guest just like in the movies," Lindie smiled.

"Are you back home for good Daddy?" asked his baby girl.

Theo looked over at Ruby again who instead of eating was just pushing around the food on her plate, something she started doing at the point when he was sharing details of his night away. "I only went for a visit, so yep, Daddy's home to stay. Ain't that how the song go; then Theo did something he had never done before; he sang a line from a song by Shep and the Limelites, "I'm not a thousand miles away."

The girls and Theo laughed but not Ruby who offered with a half-smile, "It's bad manners to sing at the dinner table. You wouldn't do that at Helen's table."

Theo let the sarcastic remark pass without responding.

10

The next morning, even though Theo had returned, things just didn't seem normal to Lindie. She wondered why her mother had not said anything to her about the incident in Dearmount, but she didn't want to push her luck. Since her uncle had promised she would not be beaten nor sent to reform school, she wasn't as afraid as she would have been without such promises. At one point during the ride home from Dearmount, she had considered grabbing the door handle and leaping out into the darkness—maybe to be hit by a vehicle and be put out of her misery. But then again, running away was one thing--suicide was never a part of her plan. Thus, after breakfast that morning, she headed to school as though nothing had happened to upset her less than ideal family. When she returned from school that day, Ruby had decided to have the big talk.

When Lindie got off her school bus and entered the house, her sisters were finishing up an early dinner.

"Why are you all eating so early?" asked Lindie.

"Momma told us we had to hurry up and eat," replied Francine.

"Okay, I'll fix my plate and join you."

"No. You and I need to have a talk while your sisters do their homework."

"I don't get to eat dinner?" Lindie immediately tensed up, and her sisters shot questioning glances that signaled something was amiss.

"Go put your things away, and meet me over in the tavern kitchen," ordered Ruby.

Lindie's shoulders drooped, but she did as she was ordered and ended up in the tavern before her mother arrived. Emotionally she was a mess—feeling tense, afraid, and nervous while ideas danced around in her head about what her mother would do and say. When Ruby entered the tavern, she started in right away, "I didn't want to talk where your sisters could overhear." Ruby didn't miss the apprehension on her daughter's face. "I'm not going to beat you. That hasn't done much good in the past."

That declaration didn't ease Lindie's fear, so she stepped back allowing more distance between herself and her mother.

"Sit down." Ruby released a long sigh and took a seat while her daughter waited in a pensive state. "This is difficult, and I don't know where to begin. Suppose you start by telling me why on earth you felt you had to run away."

Lindie couldn't believe her ears—her mother was asking her why after all the harsh feelings and words that had passed between them. Instead, she started to cry and could not offer a response right away. What could she say that would not cause her mother to fly into a rage as she had done so many times before?

"Stop crying! I'm waiting. Why did you feel you had to run away?"

After shrugging her shoulders a few times and staring at the floor instead of looking at her mother, Lindie finally spoke as tears rolled down her cheeks, "Because you don't love me like you do Francine and Vinnie. You hate me, and you've been mean to me all my life."

Ruby rose from her seat and walked toward her daughter causing Lindie to shudder and raise her hands in a defensive manner. She was conditioned to fear an attack, but Ruby kept stepping and walked over to the far side of the kitchen with her hands on her hips and her back to Lindie. For a few seconds neither of them said anything. Lindie was expecting an explosion any second, but Ruby began to speak in an almost hushed tone, "When I was a girl, my mother and I were not close. I didn't have any sisters to play with, just the one brother. I pretended the flower bushes around our house were my playmates. I gave each of them a name—people names. My brother used to tease me about that, and my mother thought I was showing signs of being not right in the head, but that didn't stop me from having my imaginary playmates."

Lindie wondered what that weird confession had to do with anything, but her mother kept talking, "You see, when you only have imaginary friends, you can make them be anything you want them to be. I told them things I could never say to my mother. I eventually gave up my playmates and just kept things to myself, unlike you. You write secrets in your journal. I know you do, so don't deny it, and no I haven't been secretly reading whatever you write. I'd be willing to bet you've written some mean things about me."

Lindie thought, *you got that right*, but she was still confused. "Why are you telling me this stuff, Momma?"

"I didn't have anyone to talk things over with. My parents were very old-fashioned. I pretty much came to accept that however I felt about things was the right way. There was nowhere for me to run away to. I decided I didn't need anybody's advice because I already had all the answers. I was really very immature even when I got married. When I found out I was expecting a baby, I was not ready to be a mother, and I still wasn't ready when you were born."

As astute as Lindie may have been about many things, she wasn't sure how to process what her mother was saying. What did it have to do with the old love letters from J? "You're sorry I was born. Is that what you're saying?"

Ruby sat back down and looked directly at her daughter. "This is going to sound awful, but yes, at first I was. As I said, I wasn't ready. As you've grown older, I think I became jealous because I see in you a strength, a spirit, a determination to hold onto your dreams. I never had that much conviction or spunk. If you were dropped off on a deserted island by yourself, I think you'd find a way to survive, but I'd drown in tears from my own pity party."

Lindie looked at her mother and could not think of a sensible response to such an admission. It was a strange mother-daughter conversation, but they were not the typical mother and daughter. Lindie had expected a heated exchange, but it didn't materialize. Ruby was hoping she had found enough of the right words to avoid her daughter delving more into the existence of J. She hoped that painting herself as a weakling would draw at least a smidgen of sympathy from her daughter.

As Ruby was about to speak again, the back door of the tavern flew open, and Theo ran into the kitchen. He directed his attention to his wife. "Francine said you two were over here. I wanna know what's going on."

"There's no need to panic. This is just a mother-daughter talk."

"That don't ease my mind none. What she say to you, Lindie?"

"Really, Theo . . . you're interrupting a very personal discussion."

"Speak up, girl! I asked you what ya'll is talkin' 'bout."

"She was telling me something about her childhood and imaginary playmates."

Theo cocked his head to one side and gave his wife a puzzled look. "Imaginary what?"

"I told you this is a personal conversation. If you leave us alone; we'll be done soon."

Theo straightened his stance and slowly backed out of the kitchen, but before he was completely out of Ruby's sight, he motioned to her with a pointed finger as though to say *remember our agreement.* Ruby knew exactly what the pointed finger meant. At that moment, she had no intention of breaching the agreement.

Ruby directed her attention back to Lindie. "He's very protective of you. There should be no doubt in your mind that he loves you."

"I believe that."

"I know I've been hard on you, and like I said, some of that was jealousy, but I need to tell you something that I've never said to you before . . . despite our differences . . . I'm glad you're my daughter. Your will and determination are indeed challenges but might be something your sisters can copy. Lord knows I hope they don't take it as far as you have on many occasions. Don't try to run away again. I'm not sure how we're going to make amends with Aunt Nita and Uncle Jimmy for that ugly scene at their house. Alvin's already called three times asking if everybody's okay.

"He was protective of me too."

"Yes, Alvin's special . . . I'll try to be a better mother than I've been to you. But you have a role in making things better also. You're just a child, so wishing and hoping that our lives can be mirror images of what you see on TV and in magazines is not going to make it so.

Nor is it going to make life any easier for us. If I've told you once, I've told you a thousand times, Lindie, we're colored people, living practically hand-to-mouth on the Eastern Shore of Maryland where we are only tolerated if we act like we know our place. True there're no police dogs chasing us down when we're in Brookville; no fire hoses set on us; but the truth is, when we're around white people, they don't miss a thing we do, so no missteps are allowed. You need to accept this as the world we live in. There's no script for how we should live our lives; we just deal day-to-day with whatever confronts us as colored people. You don't get any time off to pretend you're some other color."

Lindie looked at the floor and started fidgeting with her fingers. "Our lives would be better if we were white."

"We're not ever gonna be white. That's a fantasy rooted in simple-mindedness."

"All this time, I thought you hated me."

"I've been highly upset with you more times than I can even remember. We won't rehash those times now, but I've never hated you."

"Can I ask you two things?"

"What?" Ruby braced for the unexpected, and Lindie delivered.

No way could she ask about the man she saw her mother kissing, so she opted for a safer question, "Who was J and does he live near us?"

Ruby stood up and walked away from her daughter before mustering the nerve to respond, and she knew that lying could very likely come back and haunt her again. She returned to her seat and faced her inquisitive daughter.

"I knew him years ago before I got married. He died in a car accident three years ago. I was wrong to hold onto those letters you found. I should have destroyed them a long time ago, and I would like it very much if we never bring his name up again. The memory of him represents a confusing time when I was very young."

To Lindie, this meant that the man she saw kissing her mother was still a mystery, perhaps never to be solved, but she'd be watching, listening, and writing.

"Did Daddy know him?"

"He didn't know him."

"Okay. I won't mention him again, but I have another question."

"You said two questions."

"I know, but this is different. Can't we move to a better town —maybe to Philly and be close to our cousins?"

Ruby threw her head back in a state of complete exasperation, "Oh, Lord . . . how many times do I have to repeat myself? No, we can't move. Let's get back over to the house before your father comes looking for us again."

Since the idea about moving was rejected, Lindie thought she'd try something else as she and her mother walked back to the house, "Some of the girls at school are wearing nylon stock-ings; can I get a pair?"

"Ask me again when you turn twelve; for now the answer is no. Some of those girls are trying to grow up too fast, and I know how much trouble that can lead to."

"One last question, please Momma?"

A weary Ruby replied, "What else?"

"Do you love Daddy?"

Ruby stopped in her tracks. She stared at her daughter and wondered what else she might know? Was she being tested?

"In my own way, yes I do, and that's all I need to say to an 11 year-old about my marriage."

11

Ruby's old friend Maggie Pinkett had left Fullerton over a year ago after her husband, Charlie Pinkett, died in an automobile accident along Race Alley. Just prior to that accident, Charlie and his brother, Sammie, had committed a crime behind Theo's Place. They had stabbed Mason Jones, Fullerton's one-armed resident, who hobbled along Back Creek Road in a partially intoxicated state and smelled like a pole cat until the day he died. By some strange coincidence, or not, he was killed in the same accident along Race Alley. Charlie had accused Mason of being too cozy with Maggie.

Maggie, along with her husband and brother-in-law had frequented Theo's Place, and the brothers had helped Theo with odd jobs. But after her husband's death, Maggie and Sammie packed up and abruptly moved to another state. Since then Ruby had not attempted to establish a friendship with any of the other women who came into the tavern. Theo also shied away from establishing any close ties with tavern customers post the incident with the Pinkett brothers. Thus, he resorted to hiring random help when he was engaged in his part-time enterprises of sawing and hauling wood.

None of the tavern customers had any inkling into the current status of Ruby and Theo's marriage. The mystery man whom Lindie had seen kissing her mother was no longer in the picture. The call Ruby placed to him on the morning they returned from Aunt Nita's sent the drifting Romeo on his way. He lived on in a few pages of Lindie's journal as a man who had an interest in a fictional Sunday school teacher. Nothing seemed to stem the flow of Lindie's creative thoughts. For Ruby, the fact that her association with the mystery man had never gone beyond kissing was a huge relief now that her husband knew the truth about Lindie's biological father. As far as their marriage was concerned, Ruby and Theo were living a lie, and Theo was not handling the reality of their altered relationship very well.

A few days after Ruby's talk with Lindie, the all-but-separated husband and wife were working in their tavern (Theo's Place) packed with customers. Lindie had not been asked to help out in the tavern. Therefore, she was not there to see her parents when they were pretending to be a typical married couple. They tended to customers who were none the wiser of the reality behind their crooked smiles. Ruby attempted to keep herself occupied in the kitchen cooking, serving dinners and sandwiches, while Theo stayed out front near the counter for the most part. However, a crowd of about 10 people, not seen in the tavern before, showed up two hours before closing that night. A man in the group approached Ruby at the kitchen entrance and ordered eight chicken breast sandwiches with hot sauce to go.

"It's almost closing time. I don't have that much chicken left, but I got some pig's feet."

The man turned to Theo and yelled over the crowd, "Hey, what kind 'a place you running if you ain't got enough fried chicken for customers?"

Several other customers turned their attention to the man who had shouted at Theo. Theo left his station at the counter and approached the newly arrived group as Ruby looked on. "What seems to be the problem, Mista?"

"Ain't no problem if she fix our order. We just want some chicken sandwiches and maybe throw in some French fries too."

"Give the customers what they want, Ruby."

"I'd have to cut up and fry four more chickens, and it's almost closing time."

"Ain't we runnin' a business here, so give the people what they want." Theo then turned his attention back to the man who made the request. "It's goin' to take her a bit. Why don't ya'll have beers on the house while you wait?" Theo then guided the group away from the kitchen.

"Sure, we ain't turning down free beer."

If Ruby's eyes could have flung daggers, her husband's back would have suffered a direct hit. She hustled in the kitchen like never before, all the while cursing Theo. About 45 minutes later, eight chicken breasts had been transferred from the deep fryer, drained on paper towels, and placed between slices of Sunbeam bread. Several shots of hot sauce coated the chicken before being wrapped in wax paper. French fries were dumped into paper bowls and covered with foil. Ruby tossed the food into a large paper bag and left it in the middle of the table while she proceeded to shut down the fryer and clean up the kitchen. Theo reappeared at the kitchen entrance about ten minutes later.

"Dem sandwiches ready?"

Ruby threw him an angry look. "Do I look like Aunt Jemima to you?" She pointed at the bag and continued with her cleaning chores.

Once the last customer had pulled off the tavern's parking lot that night, Ruby let her anger flow. "Why'd you do that to me?"

"I don't know what you so hot under the collar 'bout."

"Oh, so all of a sudden you're stupid? You know good and well what I mean. I had already told that man it was almost closing time, and I didn't have enough chicken cooked. It usually takes me about two hours to clean up before we close, and tonight I had to do it in under an hour."

"They was paying customers, and we don't turn down money."

"Okay, the next time you pull a trick like that, I'll stand at the counter while you work up in the kitchen."

"I ain't never been no cook, and I ain't startin' now."

"Do something like that again, and you're going to be a colored Chef Boyardee." Ruby untied her apron, threw it on the table, and marched out slamming the tavern's back door. Theo did not follow right away. Instead, he sat down in the kitchen and rested his head in his hands for a few minutes before getting a beer from the cooler. As he slowly consumed it, minutes slid into an hour or so later before he turned out the lights and locked up the place. He knew his wife would be sound asleep, allowing him to ease into bed without awaking the dragon.

In the weeks that followed, the unhappy couple settled into what was better defined as a partnership or a marriage of convenience. It was obvious to Theo that Ruby was trying to be a better mother to her oldest daughter after their discussion, and for that at least, he was grateful. But he was beginning to miss the warmth of a body he could cuddle up to in bed. The benefits of a partnership fall drastically short in comparison to the benefits of a real marriage between a man and a woman. But Theo knew he had to persevere for the girls' sake.

A couple of weeks later after the girls had gone to bed one night, Theo told Ruby he wanted to have a talk with her in the tavern where there would be no chance of their daughters overhearing their conversation. Ruby reluctantly agreed and wondered if her husband was again going to be a custodian of bad news.

* * *

"That night I spent with Ben and Helen, I told Ben everythin,' and I've been thinkin' 'bout his suggestion for a while."

"What!" Ruby was stunned that her husband had shared her deeply personal secret.

"Don't go gettin' all worked up; he ain't gonna tell nobody."

"I don't need you going around sharing our personal business with strangers."

"He ain't no stranger; he's family."

"Family that we almost never see. You had no business sharing our situation with him. Did you tell his highcidity wife too?"

"No and it ain't just 'bout you. I feel hog-tied in this mess. Ben suggested we talk wid the pastor up at the church."

"You must be crazy! No way am I going to tell that snaggle-toothed, chicken eating, false prophet any of my personal business."

"Then what do you suggest, Ruby? You and me is a long ways from where we used to be. I ain't gonna see no head doctor. We got to talk it over wid somebody who might can help."

"You think Rev. Williams can help? I beg to differ. What's done is done. You said I could leave if I wanted to, and I decided to stay. Seems you're staying too. The family didn't break up despite your learning the truth. For your information, when Lindie and I talked, she asked me about J. I told her he was a person I knew a long time ago and that he's dead. We're not going to mention his name again."

"That don't make the truth a lie. We need a *come to Jesus* meetin' wid the preacher. I'm goin' to see him if you don't."

"You might need a *come to Jesus* meeting, but I already met Him, and I'm moving on."

"I think we should go together if we want to save this marriage."

"How many ways do I have to say it? I'm not going to see Rev. Williams with or without you and that's that . . . not about our marriage. You go if you want to, and don't bring that man to our house. I got things to do." Ruby left the tavern in a huff and returned to the house.

12

As weeks ticked by after the incident in Dearmount, Lindie continued to recover from the down in the dumps mood that had eclipsed her spirit right after Easter. The human spirit can be baffling at times, no matter one's age or the personal difficulties that periodically take center stage. The resurgence of Lindie's true character was undergirded by two factors: there were no plans made to ship her off to reform school, and her mother was actually treating her better. Therefore, she opted to focus on her school work and journal writings. Her journal mysteriously made it back to her bedroom. She found it on her dresser one morning before school shortly after the Dearmount incident.

None of her teachers or classmates had detected any change in her demeanor immediately following the Easter holiday. Having donned the face of a happy and contented adolescent during school hours had worked. As a matter of fact, Lindie was even getting along better with Francine "Meany" Mitchell—second oldest of the Mitchell girls. The two of them occasionally played hairdresser, taking advantage of the flowing locks of the porcelain-faced, white dolls they each owned. Additionally, and much to Francine's delight, Lindie taught her how to make grilled cheese and bologna sandwiches on the grill in the tavern. Relationships between sisters can be sweet if heartfelt but a toothache if strained.

Lindie's parents informed her she would only be called upon to work in the tavern if it were absolutely necessary. That was fine with her, especially since she still hated the very existence of Theo's Place as well as the stigma associated with it. She used her free time, more often on weekends to watch TV, and that fueled her cherished fantasy to one day live far away from Fullerton. Despite her parents' zero level of motivation to leave a place that caused her so much discontent, her desire to live elsewhere had not diminished. She decided she would wait until she was old enough to go to college. Trying to run away again was something she had promised her mother she wouldn't do. She would soon turn 12, and with age more wisdom would hopefully come. Maybe Lindie understood early on that *patience is the companion of wisdom.*

Change is always inevitable. Perhaps an older and wiser Lindie would view life through different lenses depending upon the situations she would encounter. In some instances, things on a broader scale, outside the Fullerton bubble, had already changed.

Although the Mitchells could only pull in a single television channel, Lindie was aware that many changes were taking place in the United States. Just the year before, the Beatles had arrived in America and appeared on The Ed Sullivan Show. In doing so, they sealed their relationship with America's teenage girls. The American music scene was changed forever. Lindie wasn't a teenager just yet, but she became a huge fan of John Lennon and the Beatles in general. She collected cards and filled an album with their photos. Her parents didn't understand the craze over four skinny white boys from another country who strummed guitars and were in dire need of haircuts.

When stories aired on television about the struggle for civil rights, Lindie paid little attention, but change was occurring on that front as well. Colored people who were subjected to the powerful forces of fire hoses and attacks by police dogs were far away from Fullerton, in places like Alabama and Mississippi—places Lindie thought she would never visit. The severity of the struggles experienced by colored people in southern states—at the hands of those who wished to permanently marginalize them—was lost on a girl in Maryland who was not yet 12 years old. She didn't have a single relative in their midst. Watching snippets of the protests on a small black and white TV at home was like watching people living in an alternate universe. It was okay to feel detached from the reality of those unfortunate people.

Other changes made one network television newscaster wonder if the country was approaching the brink of destruction. In 1965, the U.S. sent combat troops into Vietnam; Dr. Martin

Luther King, Jr. and a host of non-violent demonstrators were arrested in Selma, Alabama; Malcom X was killed, and a section of Los Angeles referred to as Watts imploded. An unprecedented doom may very well have defined the times for those on the outside looking in. When it came to many events in the United States, the Mitchells were not concerned. Life on the Eastern Shore of Maryland was protected from social and political woes by design. There was a metaphoric bubble that encapsulated the region and closed it off from the rest of the state and progressive thinkers in general.

On a very personal level, Lindie reached a major milestone in 1965, and it was a change she had to pay close attention to because she started to menstruate. While lying in bed one night, a sharp pain started in her lower abdomen. The next morning she discovered a brown stain in her underwear. She had been informed about menstruating before she left sixth grade. All the boys in the same grade were marched like soldiers in a line to the cafeteria, escorted by male teachers. The girls were left behind in a classroom where female teachers pulled down all the window shades and showed a highly secretive film. In the film white girls with bouncy blonde ponytails delighted in becoming young women. Not a single reference was made about stomach pain. Instead, the right-of-passage was glorified, so Lindie naively looked forward to her first period. But given that she and her mother had just recently forged what she hoped would be a better relationship, she didn't feel comfortable sharing her initiation into womanhood with her mother. Lindie determined that since it was her body, she would handle this new phase by herself. She knew where her mother kept her sanitary napkins, so she confiscated one, hoping it would not be missed. Without the aid of a sanitary belt, it was hard for her to keep the bulky napkin in place. Beginning with her walk from the house to the bus stop and all that day in school, her stride was awkward as she tried to keep her thighs pressed close together so the napkin wouldn't fall out of her underwear. She did not know she was supposed to bring an extra napkin for changing.

She was relieved when she returned home that afternoon, because the pain in her abdomen had grown worse. She had refused to visit the nurse's office at school. That do-gooder, dressed in white from head to toe, would have called her mother, or a note would have been sent home.

"Momma, I need to lie down before I begin my homework."

"You need to eat dinner first."

"I can't. I've had a pain in my stomach most of the day."

"Then you need some Pepto Bismal."

Before Lindie sprawled across her bed, she went to the bathroom and quickly tried to flush the used napkin down the commode and replaced it with a huge wad of toilet paper. As she hit the bed, Francine had to visit the bathroom, and immediately yelled for her mother, "Momma, something's stuck in the toilet!"

"Move aside," said Ruby to Francine. When she looked in the commode she saw the obstructing object. "What in the world?"

"I didn't do it," declared Francine. "What is that?"

Ruby quickly put two and two together. "Never mind. I'll take care of this. If you have to go real bad, use the bathroom in the tavern."

After using a wire hanger to remove the foreign object from the commode, Ruby charged into Lindie's bedroom.

"When did you start bleeding?"

A reluctant reply was offered, "Last night while I was sleeping."

"Where'd you get a sanitary napkin from?"

"From your room. My stomach is really hurting."

"You should have told me, and don't try to flush napkins down the commode again. Why didn't you tell me?"

"I was scared you might yell at me."

Ruby appeared slightly irritated. "If you're having cramps, you need a pain pill not Pepto Bismal. I'll go to the store and get you a sanitary belt and some napkins. I'm glad your father wasn't the one to find that thing in the bathroom. Napkins have to be wrapped up well and thrown in the trash.

"Am I going to have this pain every day for the rest of my life?"

"Don't be silly, of course not. Females don't bleed every day and certainly not for the rest of our lives. It's Mother Nature's way of telling you . . . you're growing up, but it's different for everybody. I'll get you a pill and a glass of water and run to the store before dinner."

Ruby served Lindie's dinner to her in bed after explaining to the rest of the family that the pain she was experiencing wasn't serious enough for a visit to the doctor. After Francine and Vinnie were asleep, Ruby checked on Lindie who was sitting up in bed and feeling better after the cramps had eased. That's when Ruby told Lindie to join her in the bathroom. Ruby removed a sanitary belt from a small brown bag and showed her daughter how to wear and secure napkins. She also told her to always carry an extra one in her purse and to change during her lunch break and after her shower before going to bed. It was one of the most serious bonding moments the two had shared.

13

As the school year was winding down, Lindie's view on things improved somewhat, she focused on things like interacting more with her sisters, meeting up with friends in school between classes, and, of course, writing. She even wrote her first one-act play for one of her classes. It was entitled, "Dream Chaser."

During one of the infrequent weekends when she did have to help in the tavern, she sensed that something was still out of joint with her parents. Resolve and acceptance had not found its way into the dicey relationship between Ruby and Theo. With their daughters just beyond earshot, Ruby and Theo were discussing something near the beer cooler when out of the blue, Theo yelled, "I'm sick of this!"

"So am I!" shouted Ruby.

The girls looked at each other, and Francine suggested that they skedaddle. As the girls were attempting to distance themselves, Ruby stood at the tavern's back door and called out, "Lindie . . . come back over here. Your father and I need to talk with you."

"Can't you ever stay out of trouble?" asked Francine.

"I didn't do anything!"

Lindie reluctantly left her sisters and returned to the tavern wondering how much trouble she was in this time and for what. In her mind, she had been especially good for a long stretch, and she couldn't think of one thing she had done that would land her in trouble. Nonetheless, she had to meet with her parents who were sounding off about something.

Lindie approached her father. "Are you two fighting about something you think I did because I didn't do anything?"

"Just hush up and listen; Uncle Fred called this mornin'. Seems that after school's out Barbara's goin' to visit her cousin in Alabama and then her sister in Georgia. She wants to know if you'd like to go wid her."

A huge rush of adrenaline consumed Lindie's body, and she felt like leaping to the sky. She couldn't believe her good fortune. Had a guardian angel responded to her biggest wish? "Yes, yes I want to get away . . . I mean go on a trip. I've been in Fullerton all my life."

"All yo' life? Imagine how long that's been. Yo' momma says things is too bad in the south for you to be goin'."

"I've seen stuff on TV, but I still want to go. Please Momma, I'll do all the chores, even cooking meals, please? I may never have this chance again."

"Things look mighty bad down there right now, plus what's already happened this year—people protesting for the right to vote," warned her mother. "You're too young to understand."

"But if Aunt Barbara's not afraid to go, it should be okay. I'll be safe with her."

"I don't think it's a good idea. We certainly have a lot of hateful white people all around us up here, but you haven't been exposed to anything like what they're showing on TV—police forcing people into paddy wagons while beating them with sticks, and they haven't committed any crimes. It's too dangerous."

"Momma, you know how I love to write. I've never tried to write about what I see on TV about civil rights, but if I'm down there, I can see for myself what it's really like. It won't be my imagination. You always say I'm just making stuff up, please Momma? I wouldn't be making anything up---just writing about what I see and hear, please?"

"We know Barbara wouldn't be in the middle of none of that stuff they show on TV, and you'd have to promise to do 'xactly what yo' aunt tells you to do."

"There, you go again talking like this has been decided. I still say no."

"M-o-m-m-a?"

"I said no. Go back over to the house with your sisters."

Lindie's face took on the appearance of a tragedy mask, her dream shattered again, as she scuffed out of the tavern. Why did they even tell her about the offer if they weren't in agreement? A chance to visit another part of the country snatched away just like that—an opportunity to escape Fullerton without having to be labeled a runaway, a chance to visit with some people whom she might have something in common with, and in the mind of a soon-to-be adolescent, disallowed for no good reason. After Lindie left the tavern, Theo told Ruby she'd have to be the one to call her brother and tell him how she felt. He also used the opportunity to inform Ruby that he had invited his cousin Ben and his wife to dinner.

"You invited that uppity woman to our house. You know she looks down her nose at us."

"Maybe she used to, but she treated me fine when I stayed wid dem."

"You didn't even ask me first."

"Cause you would 'a said no. They comin' in two weeks, and we gonna treat them just as fine as they treated me. You should bake a ham, make some macaroni and cheese, and green beans with ham hocks—chocolate cake for dessert—a nice dinner, and Helen likes iced tea."

Ruby walked away stating, "Since you're the expert on what Ms. Helen likes, you buy the groceries, Chef Boyardee. I'll fix a meal."

When Ruby returned to the house, she called her brother and presented her justification for not wanting her daughter to visit the south. She also suspected her sister-in-law wanted to get her niece away from Fullerton for a while. Barbara and Fred had not visited since the blowup at Aunt Nita's. Ruby recalled how her brother had chastised her during his last visit.

"I understand your concerns, sis, but Barbara ain't going to be involved in any of that protesting. Her cousin lives outside of Birmingham, and her sister lives on an army base in Georgia. Georgia's police ain't gonna be beating up on people on a army post."

"How come none of your kids are going?"

"Cause we got them all signed up for Bible school soon as school lets out. Barbara just decided last week to take this trip. We thought it would be something Lindie would like to do with her aunt."

"Oh, she wants to go all right. She and I just got on good terms, sort of, not long ago; but because I'm saying no, I'm the mean mother again."

"Then say yes."

"I'll think about it some more."

"Don't think too long cause we got to purchase the plane tickets."

"She'd be flying? I thought Barbara was driving down."

"No way. I ain't going. I don't want my wife doing that kind of drive without me. If you change your mind, let us know by early next week."

Ruby finally relented and gave Lindie the approval to travel south with her aunt. Needless to say, Lindie's joy was over-the-top. She didn't know a person could feel such happiness. Ruby promised to take her shopping for a few clothing items and to purchase a suitcase—something far different from the brown paper sack she prepared for her failed attempt to escape.

In the meantime, Ruby was focused on the upcoming dinner with Ben and his sophisticated wife Helen. Two days prior to the dinner, Ruby enlisted the assistance of all three of her daughters. Vinnie was assigned the task of using a rag and getting down on her hands and knees to get rid of anything that resembled spider webs or dust balls. Francine had to wash and dry all the better dishes Ruby kept in the china cabinet. There couldn't be a single trace of lint left on any of the drinking glasses. Lindie had to vacuum all the carpets and scour magazines for photos of table settings. It would be her task to set the table for the dinner. Ruby reminded Theo that he needed to purchase the groceries for the meal, and that he did the day before. He stored everything in the tavern because Ruby would use that kitchen since she would be preparing a large meal.

On the morning of the dinner, Ruby set out clothes for her daughters to wear that evening. She fixed Vinnie and Francine's hair before she made a last-minute trip to the grocery store. When she returned, she handed Vinnie a bouquet of white carnations and told her to put them in a vase with water in the center of the table. Lindie was directed to set the table, and Francine had to wash the mirror in the bathroom and wipe down the sink and commode. Then Ruby was off to the tavern; she told her daughters not to bother her while she was cooking. She didn't have to worry about her husband because he was on a trash hauling job and would return home just in time to clean up and get dressed.

An hour later, Ruby had three pots cooking for the special dinner. A stone pitcher of beverage was chilling in the refrigerator. The cornbread would be baked last so it could be served up nice and hot with butter.

Ruby had purchased some extra serving dishes that morning while in town, so she would be able to fill them in the tavern and then deliver food directly to the dinner table. With the necessary ingredients in a large bowl, she began mixing the cornbread and poured the batter into a baking pan. Just as the bread hit the oven grate, Theo knocked on the tavern door. Ruby had fastened the extra latch from the inside.

"Why you got this door locked?"

"I told ya'll I didn't want to be bothered while I'm cooking."

"That don't make no sense. Open this door."

"No. You'll just be in my way. Your company should be here soon. Go get cleaned up. It would be nice if you could show them the gardens you've started to plant. The girls will help me get the food over to the house, and I'll let you know when we're ready to sit down and eat."

Ruby didn't hear a response from her husband, but she knew he was aggravated. She looked out the side window, and sure enough he was on his way back to the house. As the bread baked, she pulled the new serving dishes from her shopping bags and washed them before filling them with the food she had prepared. She then covered each dish with foil.

Ben and Helen arrived just when Ruby had expected them. It was the first time Helen had ever visited them, and Ben had not visited since the Mitchells had moved into their new house. Helen was dressed in a navy blue shirtdress with a wide patent leather white belt and matching navy and white high heels. Her hair was fashioned in a French roll, and her bright red lipstick was in stark contrast to her pale skin. *She won't be going in the gardens with those shoes on. I'd place a bet on that.* Sure enough, Helen stood just outside the gardens while her husband and Theo conducted close inspections. After Ruby saw her husband meet their guests, she picked up the phone and called over to the house. Vinnie answered.

"I need all three of you to help me carry the food over to the house and set up while your father gives a tour of the gardens."

Ruby carried the main dish, and the girls carried the side dishes. Ruby warned against removing the foil covers until grace had been said. She returned to the tavern to get the bread and the beverage. Theo and guests entered the house and everyone exchanged pleasantries. Helen's shoes were still pristine.

"Welcome. It's so nice to finally have you in our home, Helen. You remember our girls, Lindie, Francine, and Vinnie. They've grown a bit since you saw them last." Each girl offered a timid greeting. They were not accustomed to having company for dinner, and had not heard too many favorable comments about their present guests—at least not from their mother.

"Why your girls look so clean and pretty . . . Ben and I should have visited a long time ago, Ruby, but I declare everybody is so busy these days in this hustle and bustle world we live in. Where should I put my purse?"

"Drop it anywhere you'd like," responded Ruby.

Ben and Theo stood off to the side watching the exchange between their wives. Theo was relieved that Ruby was pleasant—guarded, but pleasant because after he told her about his dinner invitation, he had doubts about how things would turn out—doubts that he kept to himself.

"Let's everybody sit down befo' the food gits cold."

"Girls, remember where I told you to sit, and mind your manners."

"Helen, Ruby's a real good cook. I hope you enjoy this meal. Ben, would you grace the table?"

"Love to . . . Lord, we thank you for this meal; we thank the hands that prepared it. We ask you for your continued grace and mercies as we go through our daily lives striving to be good shepherds in your flock. Amen."

"Ben, these dishes won't be new to you, but I thought I'd introduce Helen to a traditional Eastern Shore meal."

"Why that's very special, Ruby, but I hope you didn't go to too much trouble. Ben and I will like whatever you've fixed."

"I'm glad to hear that. It didn't take me too long to get everything prepared."

Theo was grinning from ear to ear with pride, waiting for his wife to uncover the ham and macaroni and cheese he had requested. However, when Ruby lifted the foil on the entrée, Theo was god smacked. His wife continued. "Our main dish is muskrat smothered with onion gravy. I cooked them in a pressure cooker, so you won't have to gnaw on the meat—it'll fall right off the bones." Ruby proceeded to uncover the remaining dishes. "Next we have some potatoes stewed with carrots. I simmered them down with a pig tail; you'd be amazed at how much flavor's in a pig tail. It's a dish my momma taught me how to fix when I was a teenager. 'Don't throw away no parts of the hog she said'. Helen, if you can't get your hands on any pig tails, chicken feet will do just as well. We were poor people; even fried chicken was a treat. And finally we have turnip greens seasoned with fatback, piping hot cornbread with cracklings straight from the last hog killing, and bread pudding for dessert. There's plenty Black Cherry Kool-Aid to wash it all down."

While Theo had entered into a nearly catatonic state brought on by inner rage, Helen struggled to find the appropriate words to describe the spread on the table, "Well, it sure looks like you went to a lot of trouble. I used to have a colleague from the Shore when I worked in DC. He told us about eating rodents when he was growing up. Honestly, I rarely eat meat these days."

Theo felt the need to jump in with a response before his wife could humiliate him further, "You can help yo' self to whatever you like, Helen. I should 'a checked with you to see what you like to eat. Ruby certainly knows how to pull together a meal fittin' fo' country folk. Maybe sometime you can come by and teach her how to cook what most folks eat."

"I've already graced the table, so let's get to eating. I've eaten more muskrats in my day than I can count; just haven't had any recently," stated Ben.

"I thought we were having ham," whispered Francine to Lindie who was trying hard not to break into a round of giggles.

Lindie shot a glance at Theo, and she knew he was not pleased about the dinner, but she also knew he'd try to make the best of it, at least while guests were present. Ruby's face was rigid as she looked around the table, but she avoided eye contact with her husband.

"Ruby, why don't you pour everybody a glass of that delicious Kool-Aid you slaved over," suggested her husband. "Ben and Helen, pass me yo' plates, and I'll serve up whatever you'd like to eat."

"I don't have much of an appetite, so just a little bit of the greens, and I'll have a piece of the cornbread without the cracklings," stated Helen.

Helen instantly became Lindie's kindred spirit when she expressed a dislike for cracklings. Lindie decided to share in the sentiment, "Cousin Helen, I don't eat cracklings either. You can just scoop them out with your spoon or fork like I do."

"And I don't want any tail, Momma," whined Vinnie.

"There's no tail on the table, sweetheart. I just used one to season a dish."

"But I don't want anything that taste like a tail. Tails are nasty, because they're close to the . . . ."

Theo cut her off, "God save us if anything yo' momma fixed taste like tail. There's been 'nough showin' off fo' one day. Calm down and eat, Vinnie."

And so the dinner with a duplicity of purpose proceeded. Ben, Theo, and Ruby consumed portions of each dish while the girls and Helen were more selective. Tiny servings of turnip greens managed to slide down their throats, but everyone gulped down Kool-Aid and helpings of bread pudding as though it was their last supper. At the end of the meal, Theo refused to allow Helen to help clear the table. Instead he assigned the task to his daughters.

"Ruby, I'm a walk Ben and Helen over to the tavern where I have some ice cold Rolling Rocks wid their names on them."

"Praise be," said Helen.

Ruby understood that her husband had purposely left her out of the adult beer drinking invite as a form of payback for serving his guests a lowly creature instead of the meal he requested. No matter, Ruby didn't consume alcohol, and she had gotten her point across—that being—*don't mess with me, cause I'll get you back.*

Theo remained in the tavern after Ben and Helen left. He was allowing time for most of his anger to dissipate as he puffed away on a Prince Edward cigar in solitude. He returned to the house after the kitchen chores were done and the girls had gone to bed. For certain he had some choice words for his wife once they were in the privacy of their bedroom where intimacy had fleeted away long ago, replaced by icy exchanges between two bruised souls.

While keeping his voice just above a whisper he addressed Ruby, "That was a cruel thing you done wid dinner. First time we have guests in this house and you fix dem muskrat. Is there no end to how evil you can be? What happened to the food I bought?"

"Don't start in on me. You invited people for dinner without even asking me. It's not my fault if Ben's high and mighty wife didn't like an Eastern Shore spread. And another thing, I'm not some hired help you can just order around, like you did when I had to fix all that extra chicken for customers at the last minute."

"You need to keep yo' voice down, and next time I want a special meal, I'll ask Sadie at the diner or Lindie to cook it. I don't think Lindie inherited yo' mean streak, and I hope she don't grow up to be a liar like her mother."

"There you go bringing up old dirt."

"Oh it ain't old, Ruby."

"You can stand there and preach all night if you want to, but you'll be talking to the walls."

With that said, Ruby climbed into bed and covered her head with the covers as though to shield herself from any further verbal missiles. The next day she informed her husband that when the time arrived, she and the girls would drive Lindie to Philly without him because once Barbara and Lindie boarded the plane for Alabama, she would remain in Philly for an extended visit with her brother while their youngest two would go to Bible school with their cousins.

14

The last day of the school year for Vinnie and Francine was commonly referred to as "play day." School books were piled in stacks along the walls of each classroom, and there were no lesson plans for the day. Until released to play outside, students chatted in hushed tones as some teachers peeped over the rims of their reading glasses, keeping watchful eyes on the rambunctious clusters who could barely contain themselves until released. All students had to bring their lunches from home on play day. They were allowed to eat anywhere on the playground they wished. Teachers organized games, but mostly it was a free-for-all day, but still a mandated day in order to fulfil the state's attendance requirement.

Francine's favorite activity on the playground was the sliding board. She repeatedly climbed the steps and had to keep her hands folded on her lap to prevent her dress from blowing over her head as she slid down the steel board. Vinnie favored the merry-go-round. She twirled with other students in her class as an assortment of colorful barrettes flapped against her face. Sometimes only the onset of dizziness curbed her enthusiasm.

In contrast, the last day of the school year for Lindie was not a play day. There was still school work to do. Why, Lindie did not know. Report cards were already prepared and ready to be disbursed to students at the end of the day. Therefore, Lindie assumed that lessons on the last day of school were just busy work intended to prevent idle minds from conjuring up devilish deeds. During her lunch break and while seated at the table with some of her classmates, she felt something on her shoulder. At first she shrugged it off thinking someone had just bumped into her by accident. However, when she looked up from her meal, she noted the girls across the table from her were looking behind her. She turned around and was surprised to see Franklin Elzey with a big smile on his face. "Just thought I'd say have a great summer. I'm flying out to California in a couple weeks to spend time with some of my cousins."

"That's nice. I'll be flying with my aunt to Alabama and then we're driving to Georgia."

"For real? Better behave down there, else they'll let the dogs loose on you."

Then he turned and left. Some of Lindie's lunch buddies were clearly envious. One girl had to offer her thoughts, "So you like him, Juliet? Romeo seems to like you." The tease referenced the lead roles Lindie and Franklin had played in a school play just months earlier.

"He was just being friendly."

"None of us have had an upper class boy stop by to say have a nice summer," teased another girl.

"Yeah, Lindie. You been holding out on us. Do your parents know?"

"Don't be ridiculous. I'm not ready for a boyfriend yet." Lindie abruptly got up from the table and left her classmates who were still chatting about Franklin.

15

Seventh grade was now over for Lindie. She had proven to be up to the task of handling the academic requirements, and mostly she was grateful to the woman who had made it possible for her to skip sixth grade. Her final report card revealed mostly As with a single B in music. She had not been terribly interested in compositions by the likes of Chopin, Strauss, and Bach. Classical music was reserved for Cousin Alvin in her opinion.

If never before, Lindie now possessed a one-track mind, being completely focused on the upcoming trip with her aunt. While her attempt to run away had failed in a most dramatic manner, her desire to leave Fullerton had not waned. It was the goal she lived and breathed, and it almost felt surreal that the goal was about to be accomplished. The trip south wouldn't be the same as leaving Fullerton forever and living a very different life, but at least she would get away for a while, longer than the typical weekend trips to see her relatives in Philly or Dearmount; plus she would be on an airplane for the first time.

Prior to learning that approval had been granted for her to travel south with her aunt, Lindie periodically listened, in a very cavalier manner, to televised national broadcasts about conditions in the south, especially for colored people. Other than Barbara, the Mitchells had no relatives from the south. The social and economic structure of the south certainly was not talked about in their home, nor had anything about the struggle for civil rights been discussed in Lindie's 7th grade history class.

Consequently, Lindie possessed only a smidgen of the facts. She knew she would have to take another history class in 8th grade. She decided she would take her journal on the trip and attempt to capture some personal stories that could be shared with her class if such an opportunity presented itself in the upcoming school year. Her intent was admirable, but it was also naïve of her to think strangers would readily share their sagas and with someone so young no less. Many colored people pledged allegiance to a time-honored tradition of not talking about difficult or awkward personal situations. If not talked about, issues had no impact on their lives while in denial mode. Therefore, there was no need to pass all personal histories along like griots in Africa. Colored people were experts at keeping topics deemed taboo secret and carrying those secrets to their graves. Lindie once heard a tavern patron say, "If headstones could talk, cemeteries would be a prized gathering place."

A week before the trip Ruby and Lindie went shopping. Barbara had advised Ruby to purchase very light clothing given the unforgiving heat and humidity in Alabama and Georgia during the summer. Even though Theo was not on good terms with his wife, he prepared the car for her drive to Philly—oil change, tire checks, battery, and radiator. He didn't want to risk his family breaking down on the road, especially since he wouldn't be with them. He told Ruby not to spend more than $40.00 shopping, because he wanted to give Barbara some spending money to hold for Lindie while on their trip.

As expected, Lindie's pending trip did not sit too well with her sisters. Francine was especially jealous, and didn't try to hide her feelings. "You think you're so special, but I'm going on a plane one day too."

"You probably will, Francine—next time we're at an amusement park, you can ride on the toy planes all by yourself."

Even Vinnie had to laugh at that remark, but she had something to say as well, "Me and Francine are going to be in Bible school with Nathaniel and them, so we'll have more fun than you."

"Fine with me, but I'll be a grownup soon, leaving you two behind with your pick-up-sticks and mud pies."

Later that evening Fred called his sister with bad news. The airline Barbara had reserved tickets on was going on strike the next day. Tickets were being refunded, and he wasn't sure if Barbara would try to make other travel arrangements.

Lindie was beyond crushed when given the news. She re-treated to her bedroom and didn't show up for breakfast the next morning. When Theo entered her room after breakfast, she was writing in her journal, having just finished a hastily written piece of prose about things that cause sadness, such as when pets die, homes burn down, and dreams don't come true.

"You bein' anti-social this mornin'?"

"I don't feel like doing anything today. I was looking forward to the trip more than I've even looked forward to Christmas."

"As long as you keep livin' you gonna have disappointments. What you gonna do, hide out in yo' bedroom ever time some-thin' go wrong?"

"I don't know."

"Well I know. Put that book down, make up yo' bed, and get yo' self outta this room. Find somethin' to do sides sit 'round wid a sorry face. You understand me?"

Lindie nodded in the affirmative, but that was not good enough for her father.

"I said do you understand me?"

"Yes, Daddy."

The day proceeded with Lindie still in a funky mood. She obeyed every directive from her mother and even half-heartedly played with her sisters. They jumped rope, played hop-scotch, and tagged each other around every tree and hiding place in the yard. When it was time for Ruby to prepare dinner, she assigned Lindie the task of making the mashed potatoes to go along with the meatloaf and green peas. While still in a supreme state of disenchantment, Lindie had peeled enough potatoes to feed a small army before Ruby realized it. "We're not trying to feed everybody up and down the road. Put that knife down."

Lindie had been on a fast track while peeling the potatoes, but her mind was elsewhere. She was about to sink back into a depressed mood over the cancelled trip and risk being chastised by her parents and teased by her sisters. She plopped herself into a chair to brood. Her mood was under surveillance by her mother, so Ruby turned on the radio, hoping some music would liven things up. The disc jockey was introducing the next song to be played, "Stop in the Name of Love." Vinnie tried to convince her sisters to do a Supremes impersonation, but Lindie wouldn't budge from her chair; however, Francine was game.

"I want to be Diana!" yelled Francine.

Ruby stood between the kitchen and the living room and watched her daughters lip-synch to one of Motown's biggest hits. Francine, being as skinny as she was, performed a very good imitation of Diana Ross; even Lindie had to admit that. Vinnie had seen The Supremes on TV along with her sisters many times, so she had no problem fitting into the impromptu impersonation of the R&B queens, minus one. When the record ended, the duo, with broad smiles on their faces, took a bow and Ruby clapped in approval right before the telephone rang.

Lindie answered the telephone. Aunt Barbara was on the other end. "Lindie, I have some good news. I'm still going to Alabama and Georgia, but I'm taking the train to Alabama, and then drive from there to Georgia."

"Can I still go?"

"Give your momma the phone."

"Momma, Aunt Barbara's on the phone, and she's still going on the trip—by train. She wants to talk to you."

Ruby listened while Barbara explained that she would be taking a train from Philadelphia to Birmingham, Alabama, meet up with one of her brothers and later drive to Fort Sierra in Georgia. Ruby agreed that Lindie could still go on the trip, and a day and time for her arrival in Philly was agreed upon. Ruby then asked Barbara if it would be okay for Francine and Vinnie to attend Bible school with her kids while she and Fred shared some brother-sister time together. Naturally Barbara proclaimed that both her husband and children would be delighted.

"Yeah . . . I'm so happy!" declared Lindie as she did the Twist around the room.

Vinnie joined her, but after hearing that her big sister was going on a trip after all, Francine was back in jealousy mood with her arms folded across her chest while Lindie and Vinnie continued to dance. Blessed be the ties that bind—some times.

Theo arrived home just as Lindie was mashing the boiled potatoes into what became a heaping pot of fluffy milk and butter-flavored spuds. He was pleased to hear that the trip had been salvaged and reminded Lindie not to go off the deep end. She had to behave while away from home or she'd never be permitted to go away again without her family.

16

There should at least be a few times in everyone's life when joy fills the heart nearly to the point of bursting. Such a condition described Lindie on the morning when she, her mother, and sisters prepared to leave for Philadelphia. Theo kissed each girl goodbye and offered the time-honored utterance probably used by all colored parents, "Ya'll better behave. Don't make me have to come up there. Lindie, that means you too. My pickup's good fo' the ride."

"Daddy, you wouldn't really drive that raggedy pickup to Philly?"

"Philly and beyond. Don't test me . . . Do everythin' Aunt Barbara tells you to do."

Theo and Ruby did not exchange verbal goodbyes—just lingering looks that might have meant, *I'll see you when I see you.*

As the car backed away from the house, Theo, dressed in an old pair of work pants held up with suspenders, looked on. While he waved goodbye, his daughters giggled and shouted out goodbyes in unison until he disappeared from their view. Before Ruby could turn from Back Creek Road, Lindie started to reflect upon the many times that her journal entries were solely about the desire to escape—the desire to experience some place for more than a day or two far away from Fullerton. She could hardly sit still. The realization of her biggest dream coming true was like something out of a fairy tale. Still, with the mind of a child, she had imagined faraway places to be joyous where happy people lived without any signs that replicated the backwoods life-style of her family. Then came the trip south.

17

Philadelphia's 30th Street Station was indeed something for Ruby and her girls to behold. Fred parked a few blocks from the station and retrieved Barbara's and Lindie's suitcases from the trunk. As they approached the station with its combination of a classical and modern exterior, Lindie could not find words befitting her amazement. The main hall with its super high ceiling arched over hordes of people below as they scurried about like robots. The Fullerton crew spent a little time just walking around in awe, scanning the full span of the venue, as their relatives watched with smiles of satisfaction and a few toothless grins.

"See what ya'll missing living down in the sticks," teased Fred.

"Stop it, Fred. Comments like that just feed into Lindie's belief that Fullerton is the worst place in the world to live," chided his sister.

As the adults were conversing, Lindie walked over to a lady who was selling flowers, and she used some of her traveling money to buy her aunt a yellow rose.

"This is for you, Aunt Barbara. I'm so happy you're taking me with you on this trip."

"Why thank you, sweetheart, but don't spend any more of your money here in Philadelphia."

Fred double checked the listing of departures and reminded his group that once boarding started, they'd have to make their way to the platform. Immediately following his comment, boarding for the train bound for Birmingham was announced.

Lindie said goodbye to her cousins but gave each of her sisters a hug and noted that Francine had tears in her eyes. Lindie wondered if the tears were a result of jealousy or if Francine was really going to miss her. Vinnie was pensive but returned her sister's hug. When Lindie approached her mother to say goodbye, she didn't know if a hug would be appropriate—too soon since their attempt at reconciliation.

"Goodbye, Momma. Don't worry about me. I'm going to be good."

Ruby surprised herself as she fought back tears, looking at the soon to be young woman she wished she had been. She embraced Lindie with an unexpected bear hug. With her face pressed against her daughter's head she whispered, "I expect you to do everything Aunt Barbara tells you to do, and don't try to live out any of your Hollywood fantasies while you're down south. Down south isn't Hollywood by any stretch of the imagination. Just write stuff down in that book. I know you have it in your suitcase."

"I do, and I will. Maybe Aunt Barbara will call once we reach Birmingham."

After a split second of mother and daughter gazing deeply into each other's eyes, Ruby released her grip, and everyone made their way to the platform and engaged in another round of good-byes. Fred held his wife in a brief tight embrace, kissed her on the lips, and warned her to keep an eye out wherever they went in addition to keeping St. Roger in mind. Barbara hugged each of her kids and told them to behave and to pay attention in Bible school. Lindie gave Uncle Fred a quick hug, and that ended the platform goodbyes for the traveling duo.

Barbara and Lindie seated themselves in a car where they could still see their relatives through a window. When the train began its slow crawl forward, fierce waving on both sides of the window began, and eventually the back of the last car disappeared from the view of those left behind. Lindie settled into her seat and whispered to her aunt, "I've never been happier in my whole life."

Even though Ruby didn't know anything first-hand about protests in the south, she felt she had agreed to let her daughter venture into very troubled waters. Lindie being accompanied by her aunt didn't do much to shed her mother's trepidation. However, Ruby also felt if she had continued to voice resistance to the trip, it would only have caused further deterioration to her marriage. Theo had been in favor of allowing Lindie to travel south from the start. Ruby believed his being in favor of the trip was primarily to oppose her opinion, so Lindie was serving as the perfect pawn.

Ruby was convinced that she had a supremely valid reason for opposing the trip south. Scenes that played out on television depicted a part of the country where racism was apparently the dominant religion for whites. Fortunately, most home televisions were still black and white, so splatters of blood drawn by police swinging billy clubs were not as gut-wrenching as they would have been in color. Pictures speak volumes, and actions taken by authorities who did not respect the concept of civil disobedience didn't need sound bites. Nonetheless, colored people were like so many cattle that needed to be rounded up and corralled behind the boundaries that defined their neighborhoods for better or for worse.

South of the border, civility slipped under the radar. It was an atmosphere no one in Ruby's family had experienced, but alas, her precocious daughter would soon be in its midst. One thing Ruby knew for sure about Lindie was that she'd challenge anyone who might attempt to subdue her. Perhaps it was a trait she inherited from her real father, but Ruby couldn't allow herself to dwell too long on that thought.

Instead of driving directly back to his house, Fred headed for a cheesesteak joint in south Philly—comfort food. In his mind, it was a way to lift the sullen demeanors of his passengers who weren't off on a rolling adventure.

That night, after all the kids were settled in bed, brother and sister retired to the back porch. Fred decided to query Ruby on where things stood with her marriage. "So I guess you and Theo have worked things out?"

"Worked out . . . what does that mean?" Ruby was not about to share that intimacy in her bedroom had been arrested and locked away—nobody needed to know that.

"He came back and you haven't left, so it looks like things are working out."

"He came back with some conditions. For one thing, Lindie can never be told he's not her real father."

"And?"

"And that's all I can talk about. I'm here because I needed to get away from him for a while. That's why we didn't send Lindie up here on a bus to meet Barbara. Let him stay home by himself for a while—see how it feels."

"Ruby, I don't understand why you're treating your husband like he did something wrong. You're the one who kept a very important fact from him. Seems to me you should be working overtime to make that up to him. Do you love Theo or not? Cause if you do and you keep up this attitude, he might really leave you just like Joe Tex says. 'Cause if you think nobody wants it, just throw it away and you will see; someone will have it before you can count one, two, three'."

Ruby looked at her brother and rolled her eyes. She tried to speak over Fred's bad singing, "Joe Tex would have you locked up if he heard you butchering his song like that." She got up and walked out into the backyard. "What are you treating your tomato plants with?"

"So you just going to ignore what I said and talk about tomato plants?"

Ruby returned to the porch. "Don't use that tone with me. You're my brother, not my father, and there are certain things I can't share with you."

"Okay . . . since you're not going to discuss this with me, I'm about to share something, and you can never ever tell anybody that I suggested this, especially Barbara. She'd be madder than hell with me."

"Speaking of Barbara, did you tell her, cause she hasn't let on that she knows anything."

"Yes, I told her. My wife is a sophisticated, intelligent woman, and it's part of the reason why she offered to take Lindie on this trip with her. Lindie's not one to be tied down to the sticks and the way you and I grew up. No 'mam; that girl will leave the Shore, and you can bet on that."

"Get the girl away from her mean old mother for a while. What's this you have to suggest that I can't tell your sophisticated, intelligent wife?"

"I hear tell there's a woman over on Orchid--people say she helps them with their problems. I ain't never been to her, but rumor has it she can work miracles."

"Why Fred Mitchell, are you talking about a conjure woman?"

"I ain't said nothing about no conjure. People say she reads palms and cards, innocent stuff like that."

"There's a conjure woman back home, but I won't go anywhere near her—not selling my soul to the devil. So this woman on Orchid reads people's fortunes?

"All I know is what I've been told."

"You know somebody personally who she's helped?"

"Neighbor about four houses down, Shirley, told me she helped her when she and her husband were having problems. That was three years ago, and they still together. If you don't want to talk to me, maybe go see this Edwina woman."

"I'm not going to see some mysterious person and spill my guts. Theo wanted us to talk with the pastor at Back Creek. My husband thinks preachers are holy, but I told him if they're holy at all, it's only from the waist up."

"Suit yourself; you don't ever want to listen to nobody else. Always was stubborn as a mule. If you have all the answers, why're you here in Philly for a week?

"Vinnie and Francine are going to Bible school with their cousins this week."

"Yeah right. Like they don't have Bible school back home."

"I appreciate that you and Barbara let me and the girls visit for a spell, but right now I'm tired of talking. I'm going to bed."

Ruby left her brother on the porch, but she was thinking about the information he had just shared. She knew about conjure women, sometimes referred to as black magic workers, or root workers. She had always believed that using such services meant selling one's soul to the devil in return. She wasn't familiar with women who just read cards or people's palms. Furthermore, if her brother was correct when he stated she should be working to earn her husband's forgiveness, then having left him at home alone for the week was probably a bad decision.

18

The concept of racial segregation and all of its complexities was intended to guarantee that an entire culture of people be relegated to psychological and physical dark dungeons. However, most victims of racial segregation chose not to submit to hatred rooted in the DNA of its evil advocates. Instead, many victims grappled with the problem via different pathways: in churches, in mass protests, and ultimately in appeals to amenable government officials. As a result of negotiations and people of similar political ilk coming together for the common good, one component of racial discrimination was eliminated. Segregation on modes of public transportation was outlawed in the United States just the year before Barbara and Lindie traveled south. Thus, their tickets permitted them to sit in any coach seat they desired. After the train pulled away from 30th Street Station, they moved to another car—one that was less than half filled with passengers. As the train made several stops, every aspect of the ride was going smoothly—no screaming babies, no hard-of-hearing elderly people talking too loudly. Lindie and Barbara chatted about fun family facts until Lindie asked Barbara to share more about what it was like for her growing up in Arkansas back in the day.

Barbara ignored the back in the day label placed upon her formative years and used the opening lines from a Charles Dickens novel to begin her verbal trip down memory lane. "'It *was the best of times; it was the worst of times.*' It was the best of times because my family was close knit. Sometimes people don't appreciate the value of a close-knit family. There were twelve homes along our road, and everybody was related. We held a family reunion every summer, and folks who had moved away returned home. We had cookouts, followed by games such as softball or volleyball, and then a gospel sing along. The following day after church service, the out-of-towners went back home. A lot of times, folks came back for Thanksgiving, Christmas, high school graduations, weddings, and funerals of course. We didn't have a real big family, but we could always count on about sixty people at the reunions each year. It was the worst of times because just outside our tight-knit circle, all the signs of living in the segregated south surrounded us. My parents tried to shield us from the effects of racism, but racism is like a disease that eats away at the mind and slowly sours the soul if you're on the receiving end of repeated harsh treatment, especially with no legal authority to protect your rights as a human being. It fuels the mind like an engine running on hate if a person is a bigot."

"What's a bigot?"

"It's not a good thing to be. It means you hate people who are different from you just because they are different. They don't have to do anything to you, but you hate them anyhow because they are yellow, or red, or colored, or even a different religion. That's what you've been taught to believe, and those teachings dictate your behavior."

"So that means all white people are bigots?"

"No, and that's another thing that makes being colored difficult. We have to figure out who's a bigot and who's not, because there really are some nice white people. But even when you are dealing with the good ones, you never get a day off from being colored."

Before Lindie could ask another question, the train stopped in Baltimore, and a group of white people boarded the car where she and her aunt were sitting. The group totaled six in all, and the youngest member of the group (a little girl) sat down in a seat in front of Barbara and Lindie. But she was quickly yanked from the seat by the woman in the group.

"We're not sitting close to them," scolded the woman as she dragged the girl away to seats near the door.

Barbara and Lindie looked at each other as Barbara shared, "That's what I mean when I say racism is taught."

Barbara placed an arm around Lindie's shoulders and pulled her in close as the train strained along. Barbara had not purchased a sleeping compartment even though she and her niece were in for a very long ride, so they made themselves as comfortable as possible in their coach seats. A handful of passengers boarded at Washington, DC's Union Station, but they created no excitement as Barbara watched them find seats. Lindie was asleep and still resting her head on her aunt's shoulder when a conductor walked through the car. He was making one of his rounds to check tickets. Barbara stopped him and asked what time dinner would be served in the dining car. He indicated that dinner would start at the top of the hour. Barbara nudged her niece so she could pull herself together before they made their way to dinner. After another thirty minutes or so had passed, Barbara and Lindie eased out of their seats and headed for dinner before the dining car became too full. When they reached the dining car, a colored man with a blue-black complexion, dressed in a long-sleeved, heavily starched white shirt and black vest greeted them. There was an over-sized linen napkin draped over his left forearm. His wavy salt and pepper hair (perhaps an indication of some Native American ancestry) was slicked back without a hair out of place, unlike his thick bushy, black mustache. With glistening brown eyes he uttered, "Evening ladies. Will anybody else be joining you for dinner?"

"No, sir. It's just the two of us."

"Very well; follow me please."

As the waiter directed Barbara and Lindie to their seats, Lindie took in the whole scene—small, mid-sized square tables with starched white tablecloths, each with shiny flatware and with single orange flowers resting in small glass vases at the center of each table. "Can we sit at a table near a window, Aunt Barbara?"

Barbara didn't respond because the waiter spoke up, "Sure can little lady, and what might your name be?"

"Lindie."

"So you were named after a dance?" Lindie had no idea what the conductor meant.

"She's much too young to know anything about the Lindie Hop," shared her aunt. The conductor smiled and pulled out a chair for Barbara to be seated and repeated the same courtesy for Lindie.

A half sheet of paper with menu options rested on the tables at each setting. Barbara ordered a pork chop, scalloped potatoes, and green beans along with a slice of apple pie for dessert. Lindie ordered the same. After the waiter took their dinner order, he inquired as to their destination. When Lindie responded Birmingham, the waiter indicated that he'd likely see them for breakfast as well unless they slept through the serving time. "No. I want breakfast too. Can you wake us up so we don't miss breakfast because I want pancakes?"

"That's not his job, Lindie."

The waiter looked directly at the beaming adolescent and replied, "I don't get back to the coach cars, but if I don't see you, I'll ask one of the conductors to find you."

"Thank you sir," replied Barbara.

Of course Lindie was curious. "Was I named after a dance; Momma never told me that?"

"I'm not sure how your parents decided on your name, but it's yours and it's pretty."

19

After much tossing and turning, Theo had finally fallen asleep on the sofa. He had been thinking about the current state of his marriage, but a quarrel across the road at the home of his heathenish neighbors, the Wrights, awakened him. His neighbors, who did not possess enough civility to be classified as sane human beings were at it again. He got up and went to the bathroom before he changed into his pajamas. Just as he was about to crawl into bed, there was a loud insistent knock at his front door. With bare feet he scampered to the door. He turned on the outside light and opened the door. There stood one of his neighbor's nephews with blood dripping from his left arm.

"Mr. Theo, can you help me please?"

"What the hell's goin 'on wid you Negroes?"

"Daddy and them are fighting. I got stabbed when I tried to break it up. You think I need stitches?"

"Douglas, I ain't no doctor, but step in here and let me wrap that arm." As the boy stepped across the threshold, Theo looked toward the neighbor's house. Aided by their porch light, Theo was able to see a couple of struggling figures engaged in a fist fight.

Blood had dripped down Douglas' pants and shoes. Theo rushed to get a towel to rest Doug's arm on before he ripped open the shirt sleeve to examine the wound, but there was too much blood.

"Lawd, I can't even see where you was stabbed. Let me get a wet wash cloth."

Douglas grimaced in pain as Theo attempted to clean the wound, but the blood kept gushing forth. Theo didn't know to tie something above the wound in order to slow the flow of blood. "I can't do nothin' wid this. You got to go to the hospital."

"Can you take me, please?"

"I ain't gonna do no such thing. Dem fools across the road are responsible for this." Theo pulled the towel around the wounded arm tightly and told Douglas to apply pressure while he went to the phone and dialed the Wright's phone number. It took several rings before anyone answered.

When someone finally picked up, Theo blasted the person on the other end, "Look a 'here, this is Theo across the road. Yo' nephew's over here wid a bad stab wound—bleedin' like a butchered hog. He needs to get to the hospital right away, and one of you needs to take him, or I'm callin' the law and report ya'll fightin' like wild dogs again."

"Who you talking to? What goes on over here ain't none of your got-damn business."

"I wish the hell ya'll would kill each other off, but right now, one of you better pull up a car and get this boy to the hospital. He came to me fo' help, so I'm making this my business, and I'm serious as a heart attack. You got three minutes, or I'm callin' the law and tell 'em one of you tried to kill this boy."

"Why you . . ."

Theo didn't wait for the person on the other end to finish speaking before he slammed down the receiver. He ran to get another towel for Douglas. Blood had soaked through the wrapping he'd done. When the second towel was in place and tied with the best wrapping Theo could manage, a car horn was blowing outside. Theo threw open his front door and saw the less than stable-minded patriarch of the Wright clan laying on his car horn as a way to annoy his neighbor. He didn't utter a single word as Theo assisted Douglas to the car.

With the boy settled in the back seat and moaning in pain, his uncle sped off the graveled driveway like a thief driving a get-a-way car. Theo stood in his pajamas and bare feet all the while thinking that just across the road was a house full of lunatics. So many times their personal dustups had resulted in him trying to render aid of some sort. There was even one occasion when Ruby called the law and begged them to lock up her neighbors for repeatedly disturbing the peace, but the law could have cared less if they had killed each other off. Alcohol and mayhem, fueled by ignorance, was all they knew. Everyone along Back Creek Road viewed the Wrights as some sort of subhuman clan that had unfortunately migrated to Fullerton. They had no relatives along Back Creek Road, or if they did, no one owned up to it. There was no reason for county law officials to bother with them as long as their insanity didn't impact people outside of their family circle.

When Theo returned to his house, he looked down at his pajamas pants and saw blood stains and dirty feet. He had to take a shower but no longer had any desire to go back to sleep. He checked the time and wondered how far along on her journey Lindie might be and also wondered what his wife might be doing in Philly. Foolishly, he had expected her to call once Barbara and Lindie had taken off, but no such call came. He decided if Ruby had not called by the next day, he would call Fred and make some inquiries.

Theo peered out the front door after his shower to see if a full-fledged brawl across the road was still underway, but the warring factions had calmed down. The only sounds heard came from the usual suspects that filled the night air with their various chimes accompanied by a splattering light show put on by so many lightning bugs. Theo had a flashback to his childhood when capturing lightning bugs in mason jars was fascinating for a country boy. He stood in the dark and reflected upon how much his life had changed since then. Now he knew what he could not have known as a child--that despite the poverty that defined his family, in some ways those were better days because he was free of worries.

20

When Barbara's train chugged into South Carolina, the morning sun fell on her face and awakened her. Lindie remained asleep, curled up in her seat hugging a small pillow. Barbara checked her watch and stretched out as best she could without standing. She looked out the window and noted the difference in the scenery as compared to Philadelphia. The train glided past shotgun houses—the type of dwelling where once inside the front door, one could see straight through to the back of the house; rusted trailers; junk-filled yards that matched her brother-in-law's in Fullerton, and cemeteries for dead vehicles. Lindie awakened when the train jerked to a stop.

"Is it time for breakfast yet?"

"Let's wait until we approach the next stop if you're not starving."

"When will that be?"

"Maybe 30 minutes from now. That'll give us time to go to the bathroom, clean our teeth, and wash our faces. How about that?"

"Okay."

They made the unsteady walk to the bathroom as the train continued to rock ahead. Barbara stood outside the door letting her niece enter first. Five minutes later, Lindie exited and Barbara demanded that she wait just outside the door.

Back in their seats, Barbara combed Lindie's hair and returned their toiletries to a bag under the seat in front of her. "Look out the window, and tell me what you see."

"What's that stuff hanging from the trees?"

"It's called moss. We don't see it up north."

Five minutes later Lindie asked another question, "What's all that stuff in the fields, Aunt Barbara?"

"Plants left over from cotton picking."

"You mean cotton that slaves used to pick?"

"That's right. The south was mostly built up around the cotton, tobacco, and sugar cane industries."

"But the field looks so big. How long did it take a person to pick all that?"

"I have no idea, and it wasn't just one person; it was a whole lot of slaves."

An announcement was made for the next stop.

"After passengers board at this next stop, we'll make our way back to the dining car."

Four white people and three colored people entered the car where Barbara and Lindie were seated.

"Look Aunt Barbara. There're some more colored people." Lindie was excited to see more colored passengers as she pointed them out to her aunt.

"Don't point at people. At least not when they can see you. It's rude."

The train pulled off again, and Barbara and Lindie slid out of their seats and headed for the dining car. As they passed the white people who had just boarded at the last stop in South Carolina, one of the passengers sang out loud, "Eeney-meeny-miney-mo, catch a nigger by the toe."

Barbara grabbed Lindie's hand and stopped in her tracks. She turned to face the white offender who had just insulted them and said, "Ignorance is bliss."

Lindie didn't know how to react, but everyone seated within earshot fell silent and watched as Barbara stood waiting for rebuttal from the passenger. It was a tense few seconds, but no response other than a snicker erupted from the offender. Barbara and Lindie proceeded to the dining car. Once they were seated Lindie shared, "I never heard that rhyme before."

"You're likely to hear and see a lot down here that you don't experience back home, but the Eastern Shore is no paradise either. You have to always be on your guard around white people. We won't let that man ruin our day."

"What does ignorance is bliss mean?"

"It means you're happy in your state of ignorance because you're too stupid to realize you're ignorant. Look at the menu and decide what you want to eat."

21

Theo spent a good bit of the next day tinkering with his saw and tractor. For dinner, he drove to Brookville for a blue-plate special of chicken and dumplings at the B-Bop diner where a broad-hipped colored woman named Sadie worked as the cook. She made the kind of dumplings that a person didn't even have to chew. They slid down Theo's throat like ice cream. He ordered a second plate with extra essence over mashed potatoes and kale with a side order of sweet potato biscuits. He winked at Sadie and told her she really put her foot in the pots that night. A recording of Bobby Darin's *Mack the Knife* bounced off the walls and entertained the customers who were devouring their meals. Sadie asked Theo why he was eating dinner alone, so he shared the facts related to his family's journeys.

"You was left home by your lonesome. Lawdy, lawdy. You best be getting' yo' self here for dinner every night while your wife's gone. I'm fixing navy beans and pot roast tomorrow."

"Lawd willin' and the creek don't rise, I'll be right here."

When Theo returned home, he called his brother-in-law. Fred assured him Barbara had called. They made it safely to Birmingham. Vinnie and Francine were asleep when their father called, so he told Fred he'd call back in the early part of the next evening. He did not ask to speak with Ruby.

Ruby was not asleep. Instead, she was seated on the edge of the bed, looking out the window, giving more thought to her brother's suggestion about the palm reader. *Nobody would know, and I wouldn't even tell Fred. It wouldn't be the same as going to see a conjure woman or would it?* She lay back down and tried to get in a few hours of sleep so she could rise early and prepare breakfast for everybody. That she did and set the meal on the table to be served.

Fred was the first to arrive for breakfast. "Your husband called last night to check on his family. He's going to call back this evening to speak to Vinnie and Francine."

"You got to give me directions to the church so I can get the kids there on time for Bible school."

"That's all you got to say?"

"You said he's calling back to speak with the girls. You didn't say me, so I ain't excited about him calling."

"Fine . . . out the front door . . . turn right, and walk up six blocks. They need to be there by 9, and picked up at noon."

Fred grabbed a waffle along with a couple strips of bacon while casting a skeptical eye at his sister.

Ruby had to leave the kitchen in disarray in order to get the kids up the street by 9. When they entered the fourth block up, she saw a sign in a front window of a house. It read, *Madame Edwina—Psychic,* but her hours were not posted. Nonetheless, Ruby decided she would knock on the Madame's door once she dropped the kids off at Bible school. She thought a reading could be over and done within an hour, giving her plenty of time to return to her brother's house and rest a bit before collecting the kids.

22

Adults generally acknowledge that what they don't know can sometimes serve as the genesis of difficult and surprising situations. Ruby was about to be schooled. She engaged the doorbell at Madame Edwina's front entrance where *enter here* had been scrawled in purple paint. There were four glass panes in the door where thin white curtains hung. A few seconds later, Ruby saw the outline of a figure moving about in the house, and then the door swung open. Ruby was greeted by a woman who, from her vantage point down on the sidewalk, looked like a giant. She stood about 6 feet tall. At first glance, Ruby couldn't label the woman as being colored or Creole or half and half, but certainly something in addition to colored was a part of her heritage. Her head was wrapped in an orange and purple turban-like covering, but strands of tightly curled black hair rested on her shoulders. Her eyebrows were as black as her hair while a very dark red, almost ebony lipstick coated her lips, and a heavy application of black eye liner rimmed her eyelids.

Ruby was taken aback at first because the appearance of the woman was off-putting. She thought to herself, *if she looks this way now, what does she look like for Halloween?*

"Hello, I'm just in town for a few days, and I hear tell you read palms."

"You've showed up here way earlier than most clients do. Good thing I've already had my breakfast. Come on in."

"Are you Madame Edwina?"

"Who else would you expect to find here?"

"I don't know . . . thought I'd ask to be sure."

"Indeed, I am the one and only Madame Edwina."

Madame Edwina's long, flowing orange, chiffon caftan sailed behind her like a bird-of-paradise as she guided Ruby back to where she serviced customers.

"Have a seat at that table, and I'll be right with you. Would you care for a cup of sassafras tea or chamomile if that settles you down? You seem nervous."

"No thanks. I ate breakfast not too long ago."

"Fine. I'll be right back."

As Edwina drifted off to another room, she left behind a very prominent scent that Ruby could not identify, but didn't find offensive. Ruby looked at her surroundings. Lots of pictures were on the walls, mostly of people whom Ruby surmised to be Edwina's relatives. Even in the black and white photos, none appeared to have dark complexions. Two calico cats were snuggled and resting on a green and orange striped settee just a few feet away. The shelves of a china cabinet were filled with small glass bottles, and the vanity was covered with bowls of various sizes filled with objects Ruby could not identify. Dried flowers and plants hung from the ceiling, but the thing that really drew Ruby's attention was the life-size statue of an African man. It stood in a corner where rays of morning sunlight shone directly upon it. The eyes of the figure appeared to sparkle, but that didn't make any sense to Ruby since it was clearly a statue. It certainly was spooky. The statue was dressed in a loin cloth with feathers around its ankles. It held a spear that reached to the floor in its right hand.

When Edwina rejoined Ruby, she noticed that her customer was staring intensely at the statue.

"I see you like Mozumba. It was a gift from my fourth husband. Some of my family believe I keep Mozumba to remind me of him."

"Is your husband dead?"

"I believe that to be the case, but you're not here to discuss my dead husbands."

"Sorry for your . . . losses."

"I don't waste time on regrets; you can't undo what's been done."

Ruby's demeanor stiffened. She didn't know if Madame Edwina was someone to be feared or someone who facilitated feelings of ease and comfort. Now that she was inside a den with unknown purposes, she was afraid to abruptly leave.

"Let's start with you telling me your name, or make up one if you wish. Some of my clients don't like to reveal their true identities."

"I . . . I don't mind sharing my name. After all I don't live up here, so nobody you know knows me." As Ruby spoke to Edwina, her eyes were drawn to Madame's pearly white teeth, framed by her dark almost black lipstick.

"Don't be so sure about that. The wings of the eagle spread far."

Ruby didn't know how to translate that comment either, so she let it pass. "My name is Ruby. Just Ruby will be fine. I'm in town visiting with my brother down the street."

"And what's made you pay a visit to Madame Edwina on this fine day?"

"I've come for a palm reading, but first I need to know how long it will take and how much you charge."

"Oh sister-friend, do not insult the spirits; there's no time frame when the spirits are in charge and talking to me. We'll see what you're willing to share about your concerns. My charge is $5 for the first hour. If we go over an hour, I'll adjust the rate accordingly." Edwina signaled for Ruby to pull up closer to the table and to relax while she got her cards prepared for the reading. Madame flipped over numerous oversized cards with colorful characters as the stack of bangles on each of her arms dangled against the table. As Edwina's declarations grew more and more personal, she stopped flipping cards and looked Ruby squarely in the eyes. By then Ruby felt perspiration rolling down her back as she struggled to conceal her nervousness.

"Based upon what the cards are revealing, you need a more intense intervention. Sister-friend, I've been in troubled marriages."

Ruby immediately wondered if Edwina ended her husband's lives in order to resolve their marital issues. Four marriages—certainly Ruby knew of no woman back home who had been through four husbands.

"What do you mean by more intense?"

"I have a special service for women who are having trouble with their husbands. It can last anywhere from 30 minutes to an hour, and it only costs $5 more. Are you interested?"

"Ahh . . . has it helped clients in the past?"

"No one's come back to complain," shared Edwina behind a wide grin and shifty eyes.

Once Ruby agreed, Madame Edwina instructed her to have a seat in an adjoining room where the entrance was covered, not with a door but a red draping with black butterfly appliques. The room was tiny and darker than the previous room. No window for light, but in the middle of the room was a round table with a dish that rested on what resembled a lazy susan. Edwina instructed Ruby to remove her wedding band and place it in the dish. She asked Ruby if she had a picture of her husband, but she did not. Edwina excused herself in order to prepare for the next phase of Ruby's intervention.

Ruby wondered what the woman was up to next; so far nothing had given her cause to flee. After what seemed to Ruby like ten minutes or more, Edwina returned to the room. She had changed into a different outfit—all black including her head wrap. Now she really looked sinister, but Ruby remained as steady as she could. Edwina poured a steaming liquid into the bowl that contained Ruby's wedding ring, and then she tossed in a green powder that made the liquid bubble. As vapors drifted toward the ceiling, a strange aroma filled the tight space they were in. Ruby coughed a few times. She began to think her intervention was bordering on an appointment with a conjure woman. Madame Edwina returned to her chair at the table; then she framed her hands into the shape of a pyramid and held them over the bubbling bowl. She uttered a brief chant, not understood by Ruby.

"Are you a conjure woman in addition to a palm reader?" whispered Ruby.

Madame tossed her head back and delivered a roaring laugh before responding. "I am a woman blessed with the magic touch. I don't conjure up anything. The spirits speak to me, and I just embrace my powers as a gift to help my clients. Now give me your hands."

Ruby timidly offered her hands to Edwina whose hands were ice cold. Their joined hands were then extended over the still bubbling bowl of liquid where Ruby's wedding ring lay soaking.

"Close your eyes and squeeze my hands . . . now tell me what you want your husband to do."

"I want him to love me like he did when we first got married." After answering a litany of additional questions from the Madame, Ruby was emotionally spent and had become tearful, fully taking in her admissions of guilt and regret. But Edwina was not done. When the questions ended, Edwina reached for Ruby's head and yanked a strand of her hair. From the ceiling of the adjoining room Edwina pulled down some dried herbs, tossed them in a small jar with the strand of Ruby's hair and added some of the bubbling liquid. Before corking the bottle, she once again said a few words in a language her clients never understood. Ruby was mesmerized. Then Edwina retrieved the wedding ring from the bowl and instructed Ruby to put it back on her finger. Ruby flinched because the ring felt very hot on her finger.

"It's going to feel warm for the next few minutes, but don't take it off. I don't want you to take that ring off for at least 30 days—not for any reason, or you'll break the spell."

"Did you put a spell on me or my husband?"

Not answering the question directly, Edwina offered, "This little bottle is for you, but you must do as I say, or the spell will be broken. Place it under your bed at home, and don't let your husband see it or touch it. Don't even let him know about it because that can also break the spell. For 30 days, I want you to wet your ring finger with some of this liquid and dab it on his pillow, not so much that he'll notice, but leave the bottle under the bed. You can also dab a little of the liquid on his clothes before he gets dressed in the mornings, but only use your ring finger. If you want to add a couple more strands of hair to the bottle, you can; that will strengthen the spell, but not more than 3. This takes a while, and you have a lot to overcome."

With the session now ended, Ruby paid Madame Edwina who escorted her to the front door followed by her calico cats that nuzzled around Ruby's legs before she departed.

"Meshach and Abednego seem to have taken a liking to you. They don't nuzzle up to most of my clients."

Ruby shot a questionable glance at the two cats before leaving. "Thank you Madame Edwina. I hope this works."

"If not, you can visit me a second time when you return to Philly, and we'll call upon the spirit of Mozumba. That's a longer and more expensive service."

Out on the sidewalk, Ruby checked her watch, and sure enough, just over an hour had passed while she was with the Madame. She wondered why a woman who offers Madame Edwina's services would name her cats after Biblical figures. She felt a bit lightheaded and attributed that to inhaling the vapors from the bowl. Nonetheless, she had ample time to get back to Fred's house and rest before leaving again to pick up the kids.

23

Meanwhile Theo, without any helpers to assist him, was performing his routine tasks of hauling debris. A trip to Dr. Brown's beach house in Carrollton was on his agenda for that day. The fruits of such hauling jobs sometimes were enjoyed by his family, and the major find that day was a dollhouse he would make some repairs on and have ready for Vinnie when she returned from Philly.

The beach house (owned by the white dentist for whom Theo did occasional odd jobs) was an oceanfront, two-story cottage with an attic. Cleaning out the attic was not something Dr. Brown had recently requested, but Theo thought he'd surprise the dentist by doing so. Theo knew where to find the extra key in the back of the house. After retrieving the key, he paused and looked out at the Atlantic Ocean. Standing there, he thought about the number of times Ruby had expressed a desire to visit the beach house. She often chided him for not having the will to ask Dr. Brown if he could bring his family down sometime, but it was a useless complaint from his wife. They both knew that colored people came to Carrollton to work, not to frolic along the beach.

The pull-down steps from the ceiling were easy to negotiate, and once in the attic, Theo found an abundance of items lined up against the walls and in boxes as well. He thought it was best to call the dentist to double check on what could be tossed. So much for the surprise factor. Dr. Brown was delighted that his handyman had taken on the task of clearing out his attic. When Theo called, he learned that Dr. and Mrs. Brown would actually be at the beach house later in the day to receive a delivery of furniture to replace what they had recently sold.

Armed with that information, Theo hoped for a tip if he could finish up by the time the home owner arrived. He worked with great haste. His pickup was nearly full when he determined he still had room for the addition of the box filled with knick-knacks under the window.

Theo had worked up a serious appetite once he decided to attempt a rush to the conclusion of the hauling job. He figured if the dentist arrived on time and saw a completely cleaned out house, ready for the new furniture, he'd be pleased enough to offer a hefty tip. Stopping at the diner for one of Sadie's early-bird specials would be Theo's next stop. He knew pot roast was the special of the day, and he definitely wanted some of her yeast rolls and sweet potato pie before a sell-out would likely mean a selection of something by the owner, yanked from the freezer, served on white bread, and camouflaged with gravy. Sadie had informed Theo of the diner owner's preference once they ran out of the fresh food she prepared. He preferred to defrost frozen food instead of turning customers away.

One last sweep of the attic and down the steps he went with the heavy box carefully cradled in his arms, but on this descent, one of his pant legs caught on something. Theo, the box, and all of its contents fell to the level below. His head hit a marble bust as contents of the box crashed around him, and he lost consciousness.

24

As events in the lives of those back home unfolded, the train that carried Lindie and her aunt had arrived in Birmingham. Lindie had gazed out the window and taken in all she could. She was about to embark upon a once in a lifetime experience in a place referred to by some as Bombingham instead of Birmingham—noted for its fervent strides to thwart the civil rights protests.

The intense heat quickly enveloped the traveling duo as they stepped off the train and stretched. It had been a long ride from Philadelphia.

"Aunt Barbara, it's hot and sticky—worse than back home."

"We just got off the train; don't start complaining yet. Let's go inside the terminal. I need to call home and let your uncle know we made it here safely. Then we'll look for my cousin Edith while we wait for our luggage to be unloaded."

The terminal was filled with white people mostly and not as grand as 30th Street Station in Philly. Lindie took in her surroundings while her aunt placed a call to her husband. Lindie spotted a few colored people here and there—two appeared to be attending to white children, and one elderly man was pushing a trash cart and carrying a broom.

"We actually pulled in fifteen minutes early, so Edith may not have arrived yet. Let's visit the ladies room real quick."

"Did you reach Uncle Fred?"

"I left a message at his job. Your mother must have been out because no one answered at the house."

The one thing that caught Lindie's attention at the bathroom entrance was a plaque where someone had made a feeble attempt to paint over the words *whites only.* She pointed it out to her aunt who brushed it off. "A vestige of yesterday; just do what you have to do and don't leave the bathroom without me."

Lindie listened carefully as announcements for various destinations were pronounced by someone with an accent far different from hers. People rushing past her were also speaking in a way she wasn't accustomed to hearing. "Aunt Barbara, how come people down here talk funny?"

"Remember I said no complaining."

"But you don't talk like that."

"I did before I left Arkansas. Oh . . . there's Edith at the front entrance. Don't make fun of accents down here. They already know northerners think they're backwards."

With Lindie by the hand, Barbara walked over to greet her cousin who was accompanied by her husband Ricky—a tall brown-skinned man with closely cropped white hair. The buttons on Ricky's bold blue and yellow Hawaiian shirt were about to pop due to his round gut. Edith also wore her hair cut close, barely enough to brush, but she had a beautiful round face with big brown eyes. Barbara introduced Lindie, and Ricky busied himself by collecting the luggage.

"I'll meet ya'll at the car," said Ricky as the rest of the party headed for the exit.

Lindie could not help but notice how sharply dressed Edith was in her black pants, white blouse, and black, open-toed sandals that revealed pink toenails.

"Ms. Edith, do you have children?"

"Lindie, don't be so nosy," scolded her aunt.

"It's okay suga'. No Ricky and I don't have any children, so it's nice to have other people's kids visit now and then."

"My niece has an inquisitive mind, and she can be quite chatty, but while we're visiting she's going to be very polite and not ask too many questions. Right, Lindie?"

"Yes, Aunt Barbara."

Lindie couldn't believe her eyes when Edith pointed them in the direction of a big green Cadillac. She had never ridden in such a nice car. After Ricky tossed the luggage in the trunk, he started the car and seconds later, cool air filled the car and made for a comfortable twenty minute ride to their destination. Tall orange flowers were planted along the front walkway at Edith's home. Inside was an aroma that indicated something tasty had been cooked, but the familiar humming of electric fans informed Lindie that the home had no air conditioning—just like back in Maryland.

"Would you two like to shower before we eat?"

"Sure thing, Edith," said Barbara.

Barbara and Lindie shared a bedroom furnished with twin beds covered in quilted white spreads. Barbara let Lindie shower first while she conversed with their hosts. Lindie was in awe of the bathroom filled with lots of matching appointments, but the heat felt like a heavy winter coat.

Everyone eventually gathered around a table covered with a lace cloth and began to feast upon the ham salad sandwiches and sweet tea Edith had prepared.

After the meal, Ricky excused himself, stating that he needed to finish cleaning his guns. That intrigued Lindie. She wanted to see if Ricky had a gun like her father. When he opened the closet where his guns were stored, Lindie took three steps back. There must have been five or more guns in the closet. Immediately she wanted to know why he needed so many guns.

"Why do you have so many guns?"

"Don't you watch the news up in Maryland? Never know when a peckerwood might take a notion to pay us a visit."

"What's a peckerwood?"

"Ricky Sanders, don't be scaring my niece."

"I'm not trying to scare her. These guns are our protection."

Then it hit Lindie for the first time since she had been away from home. Flashes of news events in the south crossed her mind —scenes of colored people being beaten and spat upon, whites hurling racial slurs. Here she was way down south in the place where it was all happening. She hadn't given much thought to what she might see or hear in the way of protests during her trip. She had been focused on one thing—getting away from Fullerton for a long stretch of time.

"Do they really come to colored people's houses?"

Ricky laughed, but it was Edith who responded. "This was my parents' house, and when I was a girl, the Klu Klux Klan (white people dressed in white robes/sheets) used to meet on the hill at the top of this road. They burned down our church and burned a cross on a neighbor's yard. They would try anything to intimidate us. Nothing like that has happened in years along this road, and my husband has vowed that it never will again as long as he's living here, so don't be afraid."

Oh sure. I'm not scared. Edith's information did absolutely nothing to calm Lindie's nerves. A strange feeling settled in the pit of her stomach and sent her rushing to the bathroom. When she rejoined the adults, her aunt tried to comfort her.

"Lindie, I wouldn't have brought you down here if I thought I'd have to be worried about our safety. We're going to be okay. Why don't you go lie down for a while? I'm going to sit and chat with Edith and Ricky."

Instead of lying down as her aunt had suggested, Lindie pulled out her journal and wrote about everything she had experienced since leaving Philadelphia. She had no idea how long she had been writing when Barbara called her for dinner. Some friends of Edith's had arrived with ribs and pans full of side dishes for dinner. Everyone sat out in the backyard in the monstrous heat until mosquitoes became too much of a challenge to deal with. Lindie felt a bit odd because none of the guests were her age. She sat mostly unnoticed as the grownups shared adult stories. However, she took it all in, and not one story was shared about difficulties experienced by coloreds living in the south. Instead they talked about good times when they were all kids living among relatives much like Fullerton in their segregated communities.

Lindie was accustomed to her father using a gun to frighten off dogs who chased his chickens and also for killing hogs. That seemed pretty tame compared to what Ricky had in mind for his guns. Lindie went to bed early after dinner. As she lay in bed with beads of perspiration forming on her forehead, she could hear the adult banter roll on. Barbara's brother would be arriving the next morning for the road trip to the Fort Sierra. Lindie hoped there would be some kids her age to mingle with.

Just as dawn broke, Barbara told Lindie to shower and get dressed. Edith was preparing breakfast so her guests would have full stomachs for their road trip. Grits were a food Lindie and her family were introduced to by Barbara. Therefore, Lindie wasn't surprised when Edith placed a big bowl of grits, swimming with butter on the table along with some special Alabama sausage links, scrambled eggs, and biscuits for breakfast. Just as he had promised, Barbara's brother, Johnny, pulled into the driveway at

7:30 a.m. He refused the offer of breakfast, but at Ricky's insistence he was given a tour of the garden where squash, tomatoes, something called okra, and a host of other things were planted. Lindie was beaten down by the heat and humidity, and standing under the shade tree offered no relief.

"We see you standing under the shade tree, Miss Lindie. I did that once when I was visiting, and a black snake dropped down the back of my dress," reported Barbara.

That was the last thing Lindie needed to hear. It sent her running into the house while the adults laughed at her reaction. She had not found anything funny about the possibility of a snake falling on her. She stretched across the bed where she had slept the night before and sulked.

Finally it was time for the Georgia bound travelers to hit the road, and Lindie was thankful. Although Edith and Ricky had seemed like nice people, she was ready to leave the place protected by a closet full of guns, and then there was the heat factor. No one had warned her there would be no escaping the intense heat and humidity that existed in the south. It clung to her like a second skin.

Johnny's white Chevrolet was a two-door with white-wall tires. A hula dancer swung from the rearview mirror. Naturally Lindie seated herself in the back seat. As goodbyes were shared, Johnny pulled away from Edith's house, and Lindie overheard him tell her aunt that he'd be taking the route he was most familiar with.

As Johnny's car turned the corner at the end of the road, Edith picked up the ringing telephone in her living room. It was Ruby, hoping to catch her sister-in-law before she headed out for Georgia. She wanted to tell her about Theo's fall. Dr. Brown had found him on the floor at his beach house where he was barely conscious. An ambulance was called to transport him to the nearest hospital, but he initially refused treatment. Upon Dr. Brown's insistence, Theo stayed in the hospital overnight for observation. Dr. Brown had also insisted on notifying a relative, and Theo reluctantly gave the dentist Fred's telephone number. Ruby did show concern when her brother gave her the news, and she called the hospital to speak with Theo, but he had checked himself out of the hospital. She did not see the need to tell her daughters, but she did try to reach Barbara; however, she missed the Georgia-bound travelers by just minutes. Ruby decided to leave Philadelphia earlier than planned and packed up her girls, telling them nothing other than she needed to get back home. They could continue with Bible school the following summer. Truth be told, Ruby was anxious to see if Edwina's spell would work.

* * *

Lindie found the back seat of Johnny's car comfortable, especially since she had the back of the car all to herself. She raised her window, waiting for the air conditioning to kick in, but it never did, because Johnny's car didn't have air conditioning, something Lindie learned when she asked if the air could be turned up. She then lowered her window and felt the gush of hot wind as the car cruised along what seemed like a lonely two-lane road up and down slopes. Fields on both sides of the road had been planted with crops that Lindie could not identify. They hadn't been on the road very long when a pickup truck with two white men pulled up beside them and yelled, "Move over nigger." Johnny and Barbara did not take their eyes off the road ahead even though the pickup kept pace with the car for a few seconds. But Lindie looked at the two men with crew cuts and wondered why Johnny didn't yell back. The passenger in the pickup extended a hand waving a small flag decorated with a blue X and white stars.

"Aunt Barbara, are they going to hurt us?"

"Just sit back and be quiet, Lindie. If they try anything, Roger will scare them off."

Johnny increased his speed and so did the pickup.

A confused Lindie inquired, "Who's Roger?"

Before Barbara could respond, the pickup pulled ahead and sped away.

"Your aunt's never introduced you to Roger?" teased Johnny. You better show her so she can relax. St. Roger is the patron saint for travelers. At least that's what Catholics believe."

Barbara pulled a handgun from her purse and held it in the air for Lindie to see. "This is Roger."

"Ahhh . . . Aunt Barbara, you have a gun!"

"Your uncle insists that I carry one when I travel south without him. So I was ready if those crackers tried anything."

Lindie slouched down on the back seat and stayed that way for the rest of the drive to Georgia. Grappling with the insult from the men in the pickup and learning of her aunt's gun were challenges for someone as naïve as Lindie. She would definitely write about this in her journal as soon as they reached a safe location. Lindie began to question whether the trip south was a good idea after all. She had heard and seen a lot of negative things in just a few days and wondered if Georgia would provide better experiences, because Alabama was proving to be problematic.

25

Johnny made no pit stops along the way and reached the military installation in Georgia at their expected time. The white Chevrolet slowed down as it eased pass a guard post and a huge sign welcoming visitors to Fort Sierra. Tree-lined streets, non-descript buildings, and clustered townhomes were in abundance. It was as though the fort was a separate principality. Soldiers were all over the place, colored and white—some were even walking together as though it was normal for them to be on friendly terms with each other. Johnny cruised along several streets until he pulled up behind a group of connected homes—all with brass numbers to indicate addresses. Seconds later, a high-yellow woman who looked very much like Barbara, opened the door to her home and waved at her company.

"Lindie, that's my sister Marlene coming to greet us. Marlene was followed by a tall chocolate boy who appeared to be a couple years older than Lindie. Two younger children, with complexions more café au lait than chocolate, joined in the curbside welcoming.

"Hello. Ya'll got here just in time for lunch. Come on in outta this heat. Reggie'll get your bags," stated Marlene. Reggie was the tall chocolate boy who flashed a big smile at Lindie.

"Ya'll better get your butts back in the house," shouted Marlene to the younger two kids who had started a game of tag.

The ride from Birmingham had been long and hot, but the moment the travelers crossed the threshold of Marlene's townhouse, they stepped into a different world. The cold air conditioning hit Lindie in the face like a slap, but it was welcomed. The aroma of whatever had been prepared for lunch drifted up Lindie's nostrils. Marlene's living room looked comfortable, with a couple of matching sofas that almost pleaded, come sit down and rest your weary bones. Gold was the dominant color, and photos, perhaps of family members, were clustered on a wall. No sooner had everyone entered the house, a tall dark man in army fatigues came through the back door, removed his cap, and spoke to everyone. He resembled one of the photos. It was Marlene's husband, Sergeant William Mandell, Willie for short, but he certainly was not short. Lindie had never seen such a tall person. Willie stood 6'6" in his stocking feet. She assumed Reggie got his height from his father.

A broad smile crept across Willie's face as he greeted everyone and started handing out large wedges of cold watermelon to the weary travelers, believing his guests to be parched after such a long, hot ride.

Instantly Lindie could hear her mother saying, as though she were there in person, "Watch your manners." Lindie did not like watermelon, never ate it at home, but to refuse the treat would be rude. She settled back in a beige recliner and hoisted the leg rest just as Willie handed her a tray with what seemed like the biggest serving of watermelon on the planet. Perhaps it was knowing she would have to eat so much of something she did not like that made it seem larger than the portions dealt to others. One bite, two bites, and more until it felt as though she would throw up with another bite. She gingerly returned her unfinished wedge of watermelon to Willie with a fake, apologetic smile. But an exhaustive apology was not needed because Marlene announced that lunch was ready. Everyone seated themselves around the table where shrimp salad was served on beds of lettuce along with buttery crackers and mint-flavored sweet ice tea.

"Barbara tells me this is your first time down south, Lindie," said Marlene.

"Yes ma'am. Is Georgia a better place than Alabama?" asked Lindie innocently.

Everyone laughed, and Willie said, "We'll have to see about that."

"How about if Reggie shows you a few places on the base a bit later this evening?" asked Willie of Lindie.

"I'd like that if it's okay with Aunt Barbara."

"I don't mind, but you probably want to take a nap first and then shower and change clothes. We were on the road for almost four hours."

"There's always something going on at the NCO club, but she's too young for that. How old are you, Lindie?" asked Willie.

"I'm almost a preteen."

"Then Reggie can take her to the movies or where the kids play arcade games."

"I'll be glad to show our guest around."

Lindie could hardly believe her ears. Was she suddenly thrust into a dream experience? Were they really giving her permission to go out alone with a boy? She didn't dare look to see her aunt's reaction, and since she didn't voice any disapproval, everything was okay. Aside from the watermelon, the visit to Georgia was off to a good start.

"Barbara and Lindie shared a bedroom at Marlene's, and that's where they ended up after lunch. Both needed to rest. Lying across her bed in the absolute comfort of an air-conditioned room was soothing and such a delight compared to where they had stayed in Alabama. There, a small electric fan blew hot air around the room they slept in, just like back home. In no time, Lindie fell asleep without giving a single thought to whipping out her journal to write. Too much heat certainly could bring on a feeling of fatigue.

26

When Ruby, Vinnie, and Francine returned to Fullerton, they found Theo with his right arm in a cast. Although Ruby had been told about the fall and subsequent hospitalization, she hadn't been told that the fall resulted in a break, and thus the cast. Francine and Vinnie were shocked because their mother hadn't even told them about their father's fall—not wanting to be pelted with a litany of questions she couldn't answer.

Theo was sitting on the couch watching television when his family returned from Philadelphia. The girls ran over to give him hugs that he gingerly accepted.

"What happened to you Daddy?" asked Vinnie.

"My pant leg got caught on somethin' when I was climbin' down outta the attic at Dr. Brown's beach house."

"He told me the doctors said you suffered a concussion, not a broken arm," declared his wife.

"Yeah, I had that concussin' thing too, but I'm all better now 'cept for this arm."

"Smells like something's cooking," said Ruby as she walked into the kitchen. "You don't cook, so where'd all this food come from?" Left behind from Theo's lunch was fried fish, home fries, and navy been soup.

Theo had to confess, "Sadie from the diner in town fixed that food and brung it to me."

Ruby was visibly upset. "You girls find something to do. I need to have a private talk with your father." Once the girls were far enough away, Ruby let loose, "You mean to tell me another woman's been up in my kitchen cooking for you while I was away?"

"No, I said she brung it to me."

"And how many times has she b-r-u-n-g it to you?"

"Why you care?"

"Well I'm back now, so you can just call her and let her know there'll be no more bringing it to you."

"Ain't no need goin' and gettin' yo' jaws all tight. I had to eat. When Dr. Brown asked me what I wanted, I told him some of that good diner food Sadie fixes. She don't serve muskrats."

"I wasn't gone that long. How many times has she been here?"

"I ain't on no witness stand, Ruby. You was the one who took off for Philly instead of stayin' here and tryin' to work things out."

"Never mind why I went to Philly. I'm back now, and I surely don't need any assistance from another woman."

"How's Lindie," asked Theo abruptly changing the subject.

"Barbara's just called once since they've been gone, and they were doing fine then. Should be in Georgia by now. I'm going to unpack the suitcases and get things in order around here. When does that cast come off?"

"Doctor said six weeks, maybe."

"Six weeks . . . you're right-handed . . . that means you can't work for six weeks?"

"Not no haulin', but I can stock pile some wood. Sadie said she has a cousin who can help until the cast comes off."

Ruby didn't comment, but she determined that if her husband didn't end Sadie's meddling, she would. No matter how well intended, she didn't need anything to interfere with the plan Madame Edwina had set in motion. After unpacking the suitcases, she changed the bed linens where she and Theo slept like strangers in the night, applied the moist finger to his pillow case, and strategically positioned the little glass bottle as she had been told to do.

Ruby figured that Theo being in a cast might actually aid in her mission to bring them close again. After all, he was now handicapped and would need help doing several things. She would be there to render the help, not leaving any space for Sadie or any other invader to get in the way. She'd be in her husband's good graces again in no time. Since Theo wasn't still laid up in the hospital, Ruby called her brother and asked him not to call Georgia with any bad news as it might interfere with Lindie and Barbara's time away. It wasn't as though Theo was dealing with a life-threatening condition.

27

Marlene awakened her guests so dinner could be served before Reggie and Lindie set out on a mini walking tour of Fort Sierra. Together, Willie and Marlene had prepared a feast of baked ham, collard greens, black-eyed peas, and rice. Willie shared that even when they were stationed in Korea, his wife still fixed soul food a couple of times a month. The commissary on that post was well stocked with food items that reminded them of home.

Barbara fixed Lindie's hair after she ironed one of the dresses that had been packed for the trip. It was a sleeveless orange A-line that zipped up the back. Along with her curly hair-do and new sandals, she appeared a few years older than she actually was, and as far as Lindie was concerned, that was a very good thing. Just before Reggie and Lindie departed, Barbara shoved a few dollars into Lindie's hand to pay for a movie and popcorn.

It was a strange feeling for Lindie to be strolling about after dark with a male escort. The military installation was like a small city with street lights and sidewalks, not like walking along the country roads back home in the dark. "Your family seems nice," said Lindie to Reggie once they were away from his house.

"They're okay I guess. My father can be a hard nose sometimes. I think it's his army training, and my mother sees and hears everything. What about your parents?"

"Let's see . . . my mother is in charge of everything most of the time, and Daddy usually just follows along with whatever she wants to do, but sometimes he gets mad and puts his foot down."

"They let you go out on dates?"

"No way. I'll turn 12 in the fall."

"So this is like . . . your first date?"

"This isn't really a date, and I hope I don't embarrass you."

"Just follow my lead, and we should be okay. You like Hugh O'Brian, he's the lead actor in the movie that's playing, *Ten Little Indians.*"

"He's Wyatt Earp, and that's an Agatha Christie movie."

"If you've seen it already, we can do something else."

"I haven't seen it . . . I just read a lot of magazines."

"First I want to show you the school I attend, then the commissary where we buy groceries, and the Post Exchange. We call the exchange the PX for short. It's where we shop for clothes unless we go off base. This area we're in now is an example of what most of the quarters look like for married soldiers who have their families here. Officers usually have larger separate homes in another area."

"I figured families lived here when I saw the playground. Did your parents pick out their house?"

"I don't think so. I think the army assigns housing. Soldiers without their families live in barracks, but I'm not going to take you by those quarters. Might be some whistles that would make you feel uncomfortable."

One of the other places Reggie pointed out was a spot where mostly teenagers hung out and listened to music. He indicated they could stop by for a bit after the movie.

"I don't think I'm old enough to go in there."

"You can pass for 14, and the owner doesn't card people. Only if you want to. Kids go in there to joke around and dance mostly. The owner knows I'm not a trouble maker. Do you dance?"

Lindie laughed, "Yes I do. Not saying I'm good." There was no need to mention the tavern as her training ground.

"If we do stop in, we'll have to keep it a secret and only stay a little while. I have to get you back home before it gets too late."

"Okay. One thing I'm good at is keeping secrets."

At the cinema there were soldiers crowded in the lobby, and in Lindie's opinion, a lot of them didn't look too much older than her. As she and Reggie approached the ticket window, she met the eyes of a couple of soldiers. They grinned and she returned shy, demure smiles. She felt all warm inside while basking in the attention, glad she was wearing a dress and that Aunt Barbara had curled her hair. She also made certain to walk straight, holding her head high so she would not appear too short next to her tall escort. She thought standing tall with her chest stuck out would make her budding breasts appear larger. She was thankful she had seen so many movies on television. Recalling how some of the females acted while out on dates was all she could call upon in the way of guidance, even though she wasn't on a real date. It wasn't as though Reggie had asked her out. That fact was not lost on her; he was just doing as his father had suggested, entertaining a guest, and her aunt had not nixed the idea. *I won't be able to talk about this when I return home. I don't think a single person on Back Creek Road would understand that this is not a date.* Before the movie started, everyone stood while the *Star-Spangled Banner* played. Not so for movies back home, but Lindie was on an army base. For a split second when she turned toward Reggie during the movie, she thought of Franklin Elzey and wondered what he might be doing out in California.

After the movie, Reggie and his guest made their way to The Paddock where *I'm Your Puppet* was spinning. Some kids were playing cards, others arcade games, and some older ones were slow dancing. No way could she engage in a slow dance. Such would amount to a felony offense in the opinion of her parents.

"So how was your visit in Alabama?"

"Okay I guess. We have to go back there in order to catch the train back to Philly."

"I've never heard Philadelphia referred to as Philly."

"Maybe that's because you're in the south. Philly must be a northern word."

"There's a vacant booth we can grab and maybe order a couple of sodas and some fries. It'll be my treat."

Lindie slid into the booth and could not conceal her euphoria. Being aware that some of the other guys were eyeing her added to her giddy demeanor. Reggie placed an order for fries and cokes while Lindie sang along with the next song, *Love Makes the World Go Round* by Deon Jackson.

"This is a good song to hand dance to. Wanna dance while we wait for our order?" asked Reggie.

Without hesitation, they were on the floor with several other couples. Lindie was impressed with Reggie's dancing skill, and they looked like a seasoned couple out on a date. Back at their booth, they consumed their fries and sodas then left, following Reggie's suggestion not to stay too long in a place that maybe should have been off limits for Lindie.

"At least when you get back home, you'll remember your first date and the dance. But you can't tell anybody, remember."

"Like I said before, I'm good at keeping secrets." All the while Lindie knew for sure that events of the evening would become a journal entry as soon as she found some quiet time to write, but of course, she would create a fictionalized version.

The next morning Marlene and Barbara left for the commissary. Willie was off to work, and Lindie was left home with the other kids. She played cards with Reggie and some games with the younger two kids until she retreated to the guest room to write about the night before. Her fingers could barely record the words that were flooding to mind at lightning speed. When she put her pen down, she counted the pages she had written—eight. Then she was mentally exhausted, so a nap was in order, and once again it was a comfort not to be sweating bullets while lying across the bed. How people lived in such heat without air conditioning, she didn't understand. It certainly was a luxury she wished her parents could afford, even though the heat in Maryland was a bit more tolerable than Alabama's miserable summer temperature.

She hadn't been napping very long when Reggie tapped on the door and asked if she was up to seeing more of the base that evening. Naturally, she said yes but she would not push her luck by visiting The Paddock again.

"No problem. I'm going to put some music on now, and we can all dance. How about that? But first we can watch *American Bandstand.*

Even the younger kids joined in after Reggie stacked several 45s on the stereo--*Beauty's Only Skin Deep, Barefootin',* and *The Twist.* All were having a joyous time when Marlene and Barbara returned with bags of cheeseburgers and French fries for lunch in addition to the groceries they had purchased. Lindie marveled at how much fun she was having—more fun than she typically had with her sisters whom she had only thought about occasionally since she left Philadelphia. She was living the best life she could imagine even though it would be short-lived.

"Thank you so much Aunt Barbara for letting me come with you."

"I can see you're having a good time, young lady. You know we go back to Alabama soon because that's where we'll catch the train back to Philly."

"I don't want to think about that right now. Can Reggie show me some more places around the base this evening?"

Barbara looked to Marlene for approval that was granted.

After dinner, Reggie and his guest headed out again. This time he showed Lindie the library and the building where his father worked most of the time. Lindie continued to be amazed by the number of coloreds and whites hanging out together. As they approached teens whom Reggie knew, he introduced Lindie. No one seemed particularly interested in where she came from, and that was fine with her not having to explain her origins being in a one-horse town they'd never heard of. Some of the teens did think she was a member of a new military family on base. She wished. Her tour that night did take them past The Paddock and lyrics from *Wooly Bully* could be heard out in the street. She looked at Reggie and shook her head meaning, not tonight. He understood. A stroll along a few streets where officers lived ended Lindie's second walking tour of Fort Sierra.

Barbara and Lindie had one last full day on post, and Lindie wanted to make the best of it. The thought of returning to Alabama was about as inviting as returning to the Eastern Shore. She asked Barbara if they could go to the PX and buy a new blouse and a pair of shorts so she'd have something to show her sisters that she purchased in a faraway place. Marlene had to go with them so her ID could be used for making the purchase. After the shopping was done, Marlene took them to the NCO club for lunch. Lindie was impressed with the leather booths and all the soldiers buzzing about in their fatigues. She ordered a turkey club on toast and a root beer float—yum.

When they returned to Marlene's house, Reggie was all excited about something. "Hey Lindie, my friend Calvin's having a house party tonight. Wanna go?"

"I'd like to . . . but, Aunt Barbara . . .?"

"Do you know Calvin," Barbara asked Marlene.

"He's a good kid—has a sister about Lindie's age, and their father's a Captain."

"Okay, if Marlene thinks he's okay it's fine with me."

"Do I have to dress up?" Lindie asked Reggie.

"No way."

"Why don't you wear the shorts and blouse you just bought." suggested Marlene.

"Outta sight!! What time do I have to be ready?"

"I'll call Calvin and tell him to pick us up at 8."

Needless to say, Lindie was thrilled to pieces and could barely contain her delight. She was living a dream in which the events could not have come together better if she had written the script. She applied a bit of Dippity Do on the ends of her hair and set it in rollers. She then removed the tags from her new clothes and set about writing in her journal before she drifted off for a nap.

At the appointed hour, Calvin arrived to pick up his guests. He was driving his father's red Pontiac Bonneville convertible with white-wall tires. He had the top down and Barbara Lewis'

Hello Stranger was playing on the radio. Lindie almost stopped breathing when she saw the car. It was even more beautiful than Ricky's Cadillac in Alabama. After the greetings, she climbed into the back seat. Calvin pulled off slowly and eased the gleaming two-door, swag on wheels, along several streets until they reached an area where officers lived with their families in two-story detached homes. When they reached Calvin's house, he helped Lindie exit the car on the driver's side. That's when Lindie noted that he was just a little shorter than Reggie.

The night was more than Lindie could have ever hoped for. *Where is this life when I'm back home?* There must have been at least twenty kids in the basement where blue lights dotted the ceiling. There was a table with sodas and a bowl of punch. Another table was where Calvin's mother spread out the food. A string of good music was played—*Heat Wave, Mickey's Monkey, Mashed Potatoes, and Do You Love Me, etc.* Lindie was able to keep up with every dance—guess the tavern was good for something because that's where, more so than *American Bandstand,* she watched customers out on the dance floor. Later in the evening, Calvin's sister announced that one of their cousins in Philadelphia worked for a music producer and had sent her a record that had not been released to the public yet. It was Barbara Mason's *Yes, I'm Ready.*

Calvin approached Lindie and asked her to dance. She could not utter the words that instantly came to mind. She had never danced a slow dance. Before she could say no, Calvin gently took her left hand and they eased into a stiff, but no-missed-steps, slow dance. Lindie didn't know whether to look up into his eyes, at his chest, or to try and focus her attention on somebody else. Certainly she would not let the front of her body touch his like couples did in the tavern. She was excited, nervous, and scared all at the same time. Calvin had penetrating eyes that made Lindie feel as though he was reading her mind.

Calvin sensed her uneasiness. "No fears. I'm not going to get you in a bear hug like people do most of the time when a slow song plays."

They both laughed, and despite Lindie's major case of the jitters, she did her best to relax and imitate a seasoned slow dancer. However, the intimacy of the lyrics made it hard to focus on anything but the attractive boy who had one warm hand caressing her waist and another gripping her right hand. *Got nowhere to run to, baby, nowhere to hide . . . .*

When the song ended Reggie came to her rescue. "Hey Calvin, think you can get us back home. My guest needs to rest up for her trip back to Birmingham?"

"Sure thing. I'll get the keys. Meet me outside."

Just before they left the basement, Lindie and Reggie each grabbed a moon pie to enjoy later. At the car, Calvin suggested that Lindie join them on the front seat. She didn't dare say no. How fabulously grown up she felt seated between two older boys. Calvin slid an 8-track in, and the three of them sang along with a couple of Marvin Gaye hits. *If only my sisters could see me now.*

When they reached Marlene's house, Reggie thanked Calvin, and Lindie completed her fantasy role as a sophisticated young lady. "I really enjoyed myself. Thank you for letting Reggie bring me along."

"Anytime you're back down here, you're welcomed to hop over for a visit. Hey, if we end up visiting relatives in Philadelphia at the same time, who knows, maybe we'll bump into each other." Calvin made a salute gesture instead of waving goodbye.

Lindie had so many feelings going on inside, she didn't know what to do with them. She had never been on the receiving end of such attention from boys, but she liked it.

"I saw that slow dance," whispered Reggie just before he opened the door to his house.

"No you didn't. It was just your imagination."

28

All good things must come to an end. On the morning of her last day in Georgia, Lindie awakened with thoughts about the slow dance and Calvin. Willie was already off to work and smells of the breakfast Marlene was preparing filled the house. Barbara and Lindie showered and met everybody else at the table to eat. Johnny was due within the hour to drive his sister and her niece back to Birmingham.

Lindie finished her breakfast quickly and packed her suitcase. She also took advantage of the few minutes of quiet time she had to record some thoughts about the party she had attended at Calvin's house. It was not likely that she'd see him again, and it was equally unlikely that she'd ride in such a fancy red convertible again. She continued to fill a couple of pages with memories of everything she had done with Marlene's children and her tours of Fort Sierra. She wondered what she would have to do in order to maintain the feeling of utter delight that she was currently experiencing.

The atmosphere on Fort Sierra was not a microcosm of the United States at that time. Off base and not that far away, the state of Georgia was experiencing civil unrest rooted in the civil rights of colored people being denied on myriad levels, but this was not Lindie's concern. She was pretty much a typical northern adolescent out of her element in the south. Had she been able to wave a magic wand and change the fortunes of her family by uprooting them and plopping them down in a place better than Fullerton, she most certainly would have. But as the saying goes, *if wishes were horses, beggars would ride.*

Johnny arrived on time and loaded suitcases in the trunk. That's when Lindie had to try with all her might to avoid letting tears reveal how much she didn't want to leave. It is a wretched experience to finally realize a dream deferred and then to have it end abruptly.

The goodbyes were swift, and Marlene promised Barbara a visit to Philadelphia around Christmas. Again, there were no bathroom or snack stops once they were on the road to Birmingham. Johnny shared that despite the Civil Rights Act having been passed, there were plenty of places where coloreds were not welcomed, especially in the south.

After two hours on the road, Barbara passed around some potted meat sandwiches Marlene had packed, and the white Chevrolet cruised along. They arrived back at Edith's house ahead of the forecasted thunderstorm.

Edith was tending her garden when her visitors returned.

"Ya'll have any problems—any need to call upon St. Roger?"

"Nothing we couldn't handle," responded Johnny.

"Go on in and make yourselves comfortable. There's a pitcher of lemonade in the refrigerator; I'll be in later. Gotta get these weeds from around my vegetables. Lindie, one of my cousins has some kids around your age. They want to know if you'd like to visit with them this afternoon."

"I'd like to. Do they live far away?"

"Nope. I'll call my friend later, and they'll walk over and meet you. They're anxious to meet the girl from way up north."

Lindie smiled and thought, *I'm anxious to talk to them and see what they have to say about living in this heat in a place where colored people are apparently disliked more so than back home.*

Edith and Barbara prepared dinner using mostly produce from Edith's garden. To keep from raising the heat level in the house, Ricky prepared barbecued chicken on the grill in their back yard. Veggies from Edith's garden were used to make potato salad. Okra (something Lindie had never had before), beets, and collard greens were also served. Edith was known locally for her lemon pound cake. It was served with fresh strawberries to round out the meal. Lindie had a hard time getting the okra past her tongue. She thought it was slimy but remembered her manners. *Yuck, watermelon and okra.*

She did not have to help clean up after dinner. Davina (Edith's friend) and children walked over to pick up Lindie. After the greetings, Edith cut them each large chunks of pound cake and they were on their way with Lindie following.

Edith had not mentioned to Barbara that Davina, was the wife of a Baptist minister who had been involved in some of the local civil rights protests. After two or three turns down country lanes bordered by deep ditches, Lindie and crew reached a yellow bungalow with black shutters. A large German Shepard was making a racket in the backyard where it was tethered to an iron post. A handicapped pickup on three wheels was parked on the opposite side of the house. But the thing that really caught Lindie's attention was something on the front lawn. It appeared to her as though a big plus sign had been burned into the grass.

One of Davina's daughters noticed how Lindie stared at the image. "That's where the Klan left a burning cross on our yard after Daddy was trying to help people register to vote."

Suddenly something Lindie had vaguely remembered seeing on television came to mind. There she was up close and personal with another one of the realities for colored people living in the southern United States at that time.

Once inside Davina's home, Lindie was again faced with visiting a place with no air conditioning. A couple of large fans kept the air barely at a comfortable level. All of the furniture in view was covered in plastic just like Aunt Nita's in Dearmount. When Lindie sat down, the back of her thighs immediately stuck to the plastic, and her mind was a bit troubled. The gravity of the cross burning coupled with the racial epithet from the guy in the truck and the array of guns owned by Ricky made her think it was a good idea that her time in Alabama was drawing to a close.

Davina's husband was not at home—off to visit a sick parishioner is what his wife shared before she started querying Lindie about how much she was enjoying the vacation with her aunt.

She didn't want to share her disappointment in Alabama, so she lied, "It's really been nice. We returned from Georgia this morning. It was a long hot ride."

"I know it was. I got family in southern Georgia. We usually wait until fall or winter to visit . . . Edith says you live in Maryland. Is that right?"

"That's right . . . you ever been to Maryland?"

"North Carolina is as far north as my ventures have taken me . . . you Baptist?"

"We go to a Methodist church."

"Well, you didn't come over here to spend all your time talking to me. My daughters, Pam and April wanted to meet you and maybe play some games."

"That's fine, but I'd like to ask you some questions about living in the south if you don't mind?"

Davina was thrilled at the opportunity to detail for a stranger (even an adolescent) what life was like for them living in Birmingham, Alabama. She briefly excused herself and returned with a photo album. Her daughters gathered round as she began a long and detailed explanation of all the photos she had collected, depicting scenes from the civil rights struggle—personal photos and newspaper clippings. The first few pages of the book contained her family photos from when she was growing up in the Delta region of Mississippi. Her parents had been share croppers, but somehow they were able to scrape together enough money for Davina and her sister Elvira to go to a local historically black college in Mississippi.

Photos showed a two-room share croppers' shack owned by the land owner. There was a galvanized tub with a washboard on the front porch along with two rocking chairs and a skinny cat. The couple with faces of despair were her parents. She went on to explain that both of her parents died of heart attacks while tending the land owner's crops—first her father at age 60 and her mother two years later at age 55. Both had lived long enough to see their girls graduate from college.

Davina shared that seeing how their parents struggled was all the motivation she and her sister had needed to leave Mississippi as soon as they could. Davina finished college first. She accepted a teaching position in Kentucky and only returned to Mississippi three times--once for her sister's graduation from college and for each of her parents' funerals. Her sister accepted a teaching position in Detroit and only returned to Mississippi when their parents died. Their parents left this earth never having had the experience of visiting another state.

The next section of the photo album was where Davina began her postings of pictures and newspaper articles on the civil rights struggle. She had pictures of Medgar Evers, James Chaney, Michael Schwerner, Andrew Goodman, and Viola Liuzzo, all killed by the Klu Klux Klan. Of course she had the newspaper articles about the killings and when the bodies of Chaney, Schwerner, and Goodman were recovered. Another article described Liuzzo as a mother of five from Detroit.

Lindie was getting an education on the struggle for civil rights that she never would get back home in Maryland. She had not brought her journal with her to Davina's house, but she would have had she known the treasure trove of events that would be discussed.

Pictures of colored people being tortured with fire hoses and attacked by vicious dogs were numerous. A pot-bellied white man was in the center of one newspaper clipping. The caption under his picture read Bull Connor. Davina briefly explained his reign of terror as Birmingham's Commissioner of Public Safety.

Clippings of events that led up to Bloody Sunday at the Edmund Pettus Bridge in Selma, Alabama were also in the book and of course, the aftermath of the 16th Street Baptist Church bombing. Davina shared that she knew a few members of that church who were present when the bomb exploded. They had shared with her what they described as near-death experiences.

"Why did the colored people want to march to Montgomery?"

"We couldn't vote just because of our color. That had to end. There were several white people who marched along with us."

"But why do they hate us so much? When we were driving to Georgia, two men in a pickup truck pulled up beside us and one of them called Mr. Johnny a nigger."

"I don't know what lurks in their hearts and minds besides evil. But I'm a Christian, so I need to believe that every one of

God's children has some redeeming value. Look, we brought you over here to play with my girls, and I'm taking up all of your time, so Pam why don't you and April take Lindie back to your bedroom and play for a while."

The pink bedroom was filled with dolls and an assortment of stuffed animals. April pulled out two board games, and the girls occupied themselves until the thunderstorm started. Early rumblings of thunder had been ignored while they were looking through the photo album. Then suddenly there was a loud clap of thunder, and the rain began to fall in sheets before the power went out. No more electric fans to relieve some of the heat.

Davina set up four kerosene lamps, and when she checked her watch, it was way past the time she had promised to return Lindie, but the storm was not letting up. The girls had returned to the living room where everybody positioned themselves on the sofa, fanning themselves with whatever was available, hoping the storm would pass soon. The heat was suffocating. Lindie wondered why her aunt had not called to check on her or asked Ricky to come pick her up.

"My aunt will probably come get me soon."

"Probably not. There are no street lights out here, and with this kind of heavy downpour for this long, the ditches are probably overflowing, so it's not safe to drive around here right now in the dark."

"We have to get to the train station tomorrow and catch a train back to Philly."

"You can spend the night here. Borrow some pajamas from Pam, and I'll walk you back early tomorrow morning."

"No thanks. I need to get back tonight and pack."

Immediately following that comment, Lindie issued a goodbye and bolted out the front door into the thunderstorm. Davina called after her, but Lindie ignored her. Fortunately for Lindie, she remembered the lanes she had walked down on the way to Davina's home. Sure enough the ditches were overflowing. Aided by flashes of lightning, she navigated the narrow lanes despite the river of water that covered the pavements. She was soaked to the bone in seconds, but shear fear of the storm kept her feet moving, and she ran like a track star, nearly blinded by the rain until she reached Edith's. When she bolted through the door, looking like a drenched cat, she startled everybody.

"What in the world are you doing out in this storm? I was going to come and get you after the storm passed. I couldn't call because the phone is out." Barbara was visibly upset with her niece.

"I had to get back and pack."

"That's a sorry excuse for being out in this kind of weather. Look at you dripping wet head to toe. Get in the bathroom, change into your pajamas, and go to bed. There's a kerosene lamp in the bedroom," ordered her aunt.

Lindie could not share the real reason why she raced back to Edith's despite the storm. She did not want her aunt to pack for her and possibly flip through the pages of her journal and see her entries about the party in Georgia. She just had to accept being considered a foolish child at least this one time.

Lindie towel dried her hair, applied some Dippity Do, and rolled it with the sponge rollers in order to have a cluster of curls for the trip back to Philly. Even though she had dried off, bullets of sweat quickly surfaced again because of the heat and humidity. There was no use even trying to use anything to fan with. As she lay in bed that evening, she couldn't help but think how events had turned so quickly and drastically between Georgia and Alabama. She determined that Birmingham wasn't a place she needed to visit again, ever.

Daylight arrived accompanied by higher humidity but a five degree temperature drop. Nonetheless, it was still uncomfortable. Edith's guests were permitted to shower first, hoping to use some of the hot water in reserve because the power was still out. When Johnny arrived to drive to the train station, Barbara insisted on stopping by Davina's in order for Lindie to offer an apology for her behavior.

When they pulled up to the yellow bungalow, Lindie and her aunt approached the front door where they were met by Davina. In addition to an apology, Lindie offered a heartfelt thank you for the sharing of the photo album and some of the details that defined the south as a cradle of racial hatred.

29

Back in Fullerton, Theo and Ruby continued to avoid each other as much as possible. However, Ruby was continuing with Madame Edwina's instructions. It just didn't seem to be having any kind of positive effect, because to her Theo seemed more cantankerous than ever. Ruby determined that perhaps being in a cast contributed to his demeanor. At dinner one evening, Theo made an announcement. "When that car leaves to pick up Lindie in Philly, we all gonna' be in it."

"That won't be necessary, Theo. I can drive up like I did before."

"No. We all goin'."

"Why're you being so pig-headed?"

"I ain't the one bein' pig-headed. I done said we all goin' and that's it." He got up from the table and went outside to smoke a cigar.

"You girls get ready for bed. I'm a clean up the dishes."

Even Francine and Vinnie were aware there was something wrong between their parents. Not wanting to get in trouble kept them silent on the matter.

After Ruby finished the dishes, she ventured outside to try and have a conversation with her husband.

"Theo, if only for the sake of the girls, can we please try to get along a little better? I don't know what else to do or say to make things better?"

Theo looked at his wife and asked, "You ready to have a talk wid the pastor?"

"No. I thought we closed the door on that topic a while back?"

"Maybe you did, but I'm gonna' call him up tomorrow. See if he'll see me."

"You're really going to tell that man our personal business? I bet you nobody else on this road tells him their personal business, but my husband's got to blab about our business."

"It's part of his job to help sinners and so-called saints." When Theo uttered the word sinners, he pointed to Ruby. She then turned around and went back in the house.

Her thought was, *I got something that's gonna fix you. Just wait and see.*

30

There were no moments of drama during the train ride back to Philadelphia. However, Barbara spent the first ten minutes of the trip scolding and lecturing Lindie about her rude treatment toward Davina. Lindie begged her aunt not to inform her parents. Her aunt decided that with the knowledge she had of Ruby and Lindie's relationship, informing her sister-in-law of Lindie's behavior would do nothing to enhance their tenuous bond.

The train arrived back in Philadelphia twenty minutes ahead of time. Lindie and Barbara disembarked at 30th Street Station and were surprised to see all of the Fullerton relatives. Vinnie ran over and hugged her oldest sister.

"How come everybody's here?" asked Lindie. "And what happened to your arm Daddy?"

"I fell doin' a haulin' job."

"And he insisted that we all come up to collect you like a big happy family," said her mother while smiling at her husband.

"Welcome back up north baby girl. Ya'll was treated right down there?"

"Mostly, but we can talk about that later. Does your arm hurt?"

"Not no more. Comes off befo' ya'll go back to school."

"Theo, you gonna help me with the luggage?" asked Fred.

"Sure thing, and we'll meet ya'll right outside the main entrance. Car's parked one block up on the left side of the street."

There was a lot of chattering during the ride back to Barbara's house, but Lindie was the least talkative. The reality of her return to Fullerton was closing in. She was slipping into her pre-vacation mood. She answered all of the questions that were thrown at her around the dinner table, but she didn't offer any elaborations, just matter of fact answers that amounted mostly to yes and no. Even Theo picked up on her sullenness.

"What's wrong, Lindie? Lost some of yo' tongue down south?"

"No, Daddy. I guess I'm just tired is all."

"Well you can sleep durin' the ride back home."

When the time arrived for the Mitchells to leave Philadelphia, Lindie ran over to her aunt and gave her a prolonged hug. Tears started rolling, "I'll always remember our trip Aunt Barbara. It was the best time of my whole life, especially Georgia. I wish we didn't have to leave." Then she whispered in her aunt's ear, "I'm really sorry about what I did in the storm. I won't do anything like that again."

"You be a good girl, and have a fabulous school year."

Lindie's family stood back and watched, not knowing what to make of the tearful goodbye.

"Come on now, Lindie, nobody gets to stay on vacation forever. Even Hollywood stars have to return to their regular lives now and then. You have a lot of memories I'm sure that will hold you until you get to go away again somewhere," assured her uncle.

"Come on now, Lindie. We gots to go."

Lindie walked to the car sniffling. Her sisters didn't know how to react, so they remained silent. The sniffling didn't stop until the Mitchells were well away from Philly.

"Glad you finally stopped that cryin'. If I didn't know better, I'd think you didn't want to come back home." When Theo said that, he was watching Lindie in the rear-view mirror, and she caught his glance, then looked away quickly for fear of him reading the truth in her eyes—the truth that she preferred to save for her journal entries. She remained as silent as a tomb for the rest of the ride. Perhaps instinctively, her sisters knew not to bother her. Her parents certainly did.

31

Maryland's hot and humid weather was still in full force when Lindie returned home, but it was just a hair less unforgiving than the climate in Alabama. The Mitchell girls had no more scheduled summer activities to engage in. Bible school at the local church was already over. Made-up games and general roustabout activities would fill the remaining long, slow summer days. Lindie spent as much time as possible attached to her journal. She found quiet time away from her sisters while sitting in the swing under a Chinese Elm in the back yard. There, she was only pestered by flies and the occasional wasp. The evil rooster that used to own the yard was no longer around to disrupt her outdoor writing sessions. Thankfully the rooster had become the main ingredient in a savory stew during the winter.

During one of Lindie's afternoon writing marathons on the swing, while her sisters remained in the house playing, all was peaceful until she heard her father call out for her mother who was busying herself in the tavern.

"Ruby! Get over here right now and I mean right now!"

Lindie let her feet drag the ground and eased the swing to a stop. Something was seriously wrong, because her father had to be really upset to use the tone she was hearing. She had been at the receiving end of his anger when he caught her trying to run away. This time she was glad she wasn't the reason for his anger, and she would not rush into the house to see what was going on. No, she would be as detached as possible, and let someone else suffer the consequences of their misguided behavior. She waited with bated breath and both hands clutching her journal to see whatever was about to unfold.

Ruby appeared at the back door of the tavern and responded, "What do you want? I'm busy!"

Lindie could not see from her vantage point, but in response to his wife, Theo held up a little glass bottle. Apparently while playing around in the house with Francine, Vinnie found the bottle, delivered it to her father, and asked him if she could have it. Theo figured that the only family member who likely knew the significance of the little glass bottle was his wife, so he was calling her on it.

Fearing some sort of confrontation, Vinnie and Francine ran out the back door of the house and joined Lindie in the back yard.

"Why's Daddy upset?" asked Lindie of her sisters.

"I found a bottle under their bed, and when I asked Daddy if I could have it, he grabbed it and started calling for Momma."

Ruby saw the bottle in her husband's hand and absolutely could not believe it. *O Lord she uttered to herself,* as she took a few steps away from the tavern.

"You gonna come over here and explain this, or do I have to come over there?"

Having been raised in the country, Theo had a suspicion about the bottle his baby girl had found. Something told him his wife would know of its origin.

The girls were all ears, trying to figure out why the fuss over a little bottle. Meanwhile Ruby walked over to the house.

"Let's sneak in the back door and listen," suggested Francine.

"Not me, Daddy's really mad about something. You two go if you want to," said Lindie.

"I'm staying with Lindie," offered Vinnie.

"Chickens, both of you. If I find out what's wrong, see if I tell you anything!" With that said, Francine darted for the house. Her sisters watched as she tipped up the back steps and eased through the screen door. Lindie and Vinnie waited in the back yard, not knowing what to expect next, but they didn't have to wait too long.

"You said you found the bottle under their bed?" asked Lindie.

"Yeah. It's got some water and hairs in it."

"That sounds strange. I didn't put it there. Did Francine put it there?"

"I don't think so. She would 'a told me if she had."

As soon as Ruby had returned to the house, Theo ushered her into the living room and closed the front door. He didn't want the Wrights to hear him fussing at his wife. "I'm a give you a chance to tell me what this is befo' I tell you what I think it is, so start talkin'."

Ruby decided to stand her ground. With her hands resting on her hips she responded, "Don't talk to me like I'm a child, Theo Lindell Mitchell."

"All right, you had yo' chance. This here looks like to me you had some kind 'a spell put on this house or was it for me?"

"If it was a spell on you, it sure hasn't worked has it? So stop jumping to conclusions."

"Okay, let me ask the question 'nother way. Did you put this bottle under our bed, and I don't want no philosophizin', just a yes or no."

After thinking for a second Ruby shifted from confrontational to a stance of defiance and decided to come clean. What did she have to loose—certainly not a loving relationship with her husband, "Yes, I put it there."

That's when the warring couple heard snickering in the kitchen. Ruby burst into the kitchen and chased an interloping Francine out the back door. Vinnie and Lindie huddled at their safe location away from the melee and were thankful they had not followed Francine's suggestion to assume the roles of sleuths. "You know better than to be spying on your parents' private conversations. I'm deal with you later," yelled Ruby to Francine's back as she continued to run toward her sisters.

Ruby closed the back door, and continued her conversation with her husband. "You told me if our marriage was going to survive, we needed help, but I wasn't willing to talk to the pastor. I told you that, so I don't know why you're upset that I tried something else. At least I'm trying. What' have you done?"

"What I done is let you stay here."

"Negro, you haven't l-e-t me stay anywhere! This was my house long before you came along, need I remind you?"

Theo held up the bottle. "What's this, Ruby, and where'd it come from?"

"If you must know, I got it from a woman while I was in Philadelphia. I was supposed to give it 30 days to bring us closer together. Like I said, I was trying."

"Well, I ain't in favor of how you was tryin' wid no voo-doo who-doo stuff."

"It's not voo-doo."

"It sure ain't nothin' a Christian person would do. You seem hell-bent on goin' from bad to worse. Wait till I tell yo' brother."

"He's the one who told me about the woman."

Theo extended his hand with the bottle to his wife. "This is goin' in the trash, and I want to see you throw it away. My sister will have a field day laughin' 'bout this."

Ruby snatched the bottle from Theo's hand. "Why do you have to tell her anything about this?"

"Okay . . . you don't want her to know . . . then you'll go wid me to talk wid the preacher."

Ruby threw the bottle in the kitchen trash can and sank into a chair knowing that her under-handed attempt to bring about a degree of reconciliation had suffered a humiliating defeat. She might have to disclose her worse deed to the snaggled-toothed Rev. Williams after all. Theo walked out to the backyard to have a talk with his daughters.

"Oh, no, here comes Daddy," said Vinnie as she and her sisters straightened their stances and prepared for what, they didn't know.

"Ms. Francine, you never cease to amaze me wid yo' gull. Sneakin' in to hear yo' parents' private conversation. Ain't you been taught better?" Theo didn't give her a chance to answer. "I got somethin' for all ya'll, so you'll never forget this lesson. To-morrow morning, I want you up by 6 and dressed in your workin' clothes, and you'll need yo' straw hats."

"What're you going to have us do?" inquired an agitated Lindie.

"Never you mind now. Ya'll find out tomorrow mornin'."

"But Daddy, if it's going to be some kind of punishment, I didn't do anything."

"No sassin' or I'll come up wid somethin' extra." Theo turned and walked back to the house where he and his wife continued a private conversation.

The girls were left in the back yard, perplexed. Lindie was steamed. "I swear, Francine you get us into trouble over and over with your tremendously stupid ideas. I wish you weren't my sister."

"And I wish you weren't mine."

"Stop it before Daddy hears you and comes out here again," pleaded Vinnie.

"And you, little Miss Muffet should have stayed on your tuffet instead of searching around on a scavenger hunt and finding that bottle. I'm going to the tavern to be by myself. Why did I have to leave Fort Sierra?" Lindie ran away leaving her sisters behind.

Meanwhile, Ruby and Theo had a very intense heart to heart in the privacy of their living room, confident in the fact that no one was listening. Ruby responded to Theo's questions about who, what, where, when, and why she had enlisted the aid of Madame Edwina. During most of her explanation, Theo just sat shaking his head, but despite Ruby having been better educated that he, at the end of her litany of explanations, he responded, having given much thought to all she had shared.

"Ruby, we're either gonna bring an end to this nonsense or we ain't. Nothin' you can say will change the fact that you chose to hide somethin' really important from me and kept it a secret all des years—nothin'. The truth can get old, but it don't never die. You can try and come up wid all the schemes you want, but when are you really gonna start to try and save this marriage? Matter of fact, I ain't sure you really want to. Yeah, you been helpin' me since I got this cast on, but that don't take a wife. Do you want to be here, or you got dreams like Lindie of goin' off somewhere and livin' a different life wid somebody else?"

Perhaps from exhaustion over the entire ordeal beginning with the high drama in Dearmount up until then, Ruby was burdened with guilt and fatigue. "I think part of my problem with Lindie had been that I envied her spirit and willingness to express her feelings so freely. Yes, there have indeed been times when I wanted to run away from this life and move on, but I never attempted to make any solid plans to do so. As I sit here now, I think it's because I know this is where I belong and where I want to be. I've witnessed a lot of trifling men come into that tavern, and I know you're not like them. Sometimes I think God gave me a second chance when I married you, even though you might find that hard to believe. I've not been perfect, and you're not perfect, but I really didn't start out our marriage trying to hurt you. I hope one day you will believe me."

"I ain't ready to believe yet, but tell you what, I did tell the pastor that we were havin' some problems."

Ruby's head dropped to her chest.

"Hold up. If you don't want to talk wid Rev. Williams, there's a guest preacher comin' next Sunday. Can't we talk to him? Then you won't have to worry 'bout Williams givin' you the stink-eye whenever you see him."

Ruby stared at her husband, contemplating her response, "Fine. Tell Rev. Williams we want to talk with the guest pastor, but not at the church—here with the doors locked and the girls outside."

"Amen. Thank you Jesus!"

"Are we done for now? I have more work to do in the tavern."

"Yep, and I need for you to not interfere wid what I got planned fo' the girls tomorrow mornin'. Don't ask me what it is. You'll find out when they find out."

32

Theo awakened Ruby at 5 a.m. the next morning and requested that she fix an early breakfast for the girls, because they would need fuel to energize them for the day ahead. Ruby did as requested, while her husband rounded up the still sleepy trio.

First he knocked on the door to the room shared by Vinnie and Francine. "Time to get up and get dressed. Momma's fixin' breakfast right now." Then he strolled over to Lindie's room. She was already awake, having heard him banging on her sisters' door, but not wanting to appear eager, she waited for him to knock on her's. "Why do we have to get up so early? We're on summer break."

"Ya'll got ten minutes to get to the breakfast table."

Vinnie was fussing at Francine, still labeling her as the reason for whatever punishment was coming.

"I just wanted to know what they were talking about."

"I said get dressed and stop all that yakkin'."

Ruby finally asked her husband what he had planned that required the girls to get up so early. "Are we going somewhere?"

"You ain't, but they are."

After breakfast, Theo ordered the girls to climb onto the back of his pickup and be seated. He cranked up the engine and delivered his daughters to a field where about 30 acres of tomatoes had been planted by a local farmer. Some migrant pickers were already there, having arrived early to select their rows. The scene was like a throwback to plantation days. Migrants, with their backs bent, wore straw hats or had their heads wrapped in an assortment of rags.

Lindie was the first to protest once Theo parked his pickup, "Oh no, I don't believe this. Daddy, are you really going to make us work in that field like slaves?" That comment was overheard by some of the migrant workers who then shot inquisitive glances at the Mitchells.

"A little hard work ain't never kilt nobody. You get paid for what you pick."

"Daddy, I didn't do anything to deserve this. Francine's the one who sneaked in the house," reminded Lindie.

"It don't matter. I should 'a done this a long time ago—teachin' ya'll what it means to really earn some money. You can buy some note paper and pencils for school wid the money you earn."

"I could 'a been paid for helping Momma in the tavern instead of this."

"If you keep up the sass talk, you could be back here for a week instead of just today."

Lindie was mad enough to spit fire. Vinnie's lower lip was poked out while Francine remained stoic. Theo's threat of a possible week at field-hand work was the only thing that kept Lindie's temper under control. She looked at Francine and wanted to throw her off the truck.

"Get down from the truck and I'll tell you what rows to pick soon as I get some baskets fo' you to fill."

At that hour of the day, the sun was already shining bright, and the temperature was forecasted to reach the high 80s with a chance of severe thunderstorms later in the day.

Vinnie asked, "How many baskets do we have to pick, Daddy? What if we have to go to the bathroom?"

"Fill as many baskets as you can and leave them in between the rows as you work. I'll come back later and help you round'em up. Ain't no bathroom out here, just dem weeds behind the trees over there."

"I wish I'd stayed in Georgia."

"Ummm hmmm, that's one reason why you're out here now. You been actin' like you never wanted to come back home. I remember dem tears you cried when we left Philly."

"See. I'm not the only reason we're out here," remarked Francine.

"Well, I didn't do anything, so can I go back home?" asked Vinnie.

"This lesson is a one-for-all and all-for-one, so no, you workin' here wid yo' sisters. Ya'll remember this one day when you all growed up."

"If we don't die out here first," mumbled Lindie.

"What'd you say?"

"Nothing!"

"Here the baskets, and watch how I pull these tomatoes off the vine. Just pick the ones that're ripe. You don't get paid for pickin' the green ones. Now get to work; I'll be back later to check on you, and don't let me come back here and find there's been some kind 'a dust up, else there's gonna be some serious be-hind whippin' back home."

Theo drove off the field and headed back home leaving the girls, who adjusted their straw hats and began the experience of back-breaking field work. The migrants in the field ignored them after Theo departed.

After about twenty minutes of picking, Vinnie declared that something had bitten her. When she showed her redden finger to Lindie, she was advised to just keep picking. "You better get back over in your row and forget about whatever you think bit you. I don't intend to come back here again because you're claiming some imaginary bug bit you."

"But something did bite me, and it hurts."

"I don't care! Get away from me!!" screamed Lindie drawing the attention of those around her. Vinnie started crying but re-turned to her row and eventually continued to pick though she was partially blinded by her tears. Francine didn't utter a word, not even when she saw her big sister glaring at her with utter disgust.

After Theo left the field, he returned home and explained to Ruby what he had done.

"You did what?" Ruby was shocked. "They don't know anything about field work, and I can't believe you just left them there by themselves."

"They be all right."

"Are you gonna let them keep the money they earn?"

"Yep. That's part of the lesson."

One hour, two hours, and then five and a half hours passed before Theo returned to the field. It had always been his intention to collect his girls around lunch time. When Lindie saw her father's pickup return to the field, she didn't even bother to signal her sisters. Instead, she ran over to him. "Daddy, can we go home now, please? It's hot out here, and now I'm all dirty from crawling in the dirt. Plus, I'm getting a sun tan."

"Depends. If you think you can help yo' sistas count up their baskets so you can get paid, then we can go."

Without responding, Lindie ran to her sisters with the news that propelled them into rapid action. Theo walked over to the platform and watched as the girls collected their meager earnings. Francine earned $3.00, Vinnie $1.50, and Lindie $4.00. All were quiet during the ride home, nursing degrees of dismay and attitude plus one swollen finger.

Ruby was standing at the front door when Theo returned with their reluctant field hands. Lindie ran past her mother in order to be the first to shower. Meanwhile, Vinnie began to share the details of how she had been bitten.

"Momma, see my finger. A bug bit me. When I told Lindie she yelled at me. It still hurts."

"Let me see." Ruby examined the finger. "It does look swollen. What bit you?"

"It was a green bug with red eyes."

"I ain't never heared of no green bug wid red eyes."

Francine doubled over in laughter, and it was difficult for Ruby to keep a straight face.

"It was too."

"Okay. Momma's gonna make it all better. You can get in the shower when Lindie's done, and we'll take care of that finger."

Lindie let the shower water drench her from head to toe while trying to allow some of her anger to subside before she rejoined her family. It didn't even matter to her whether her mother would be willing to press her hair out after the impromptu shampoo or not. She needed to wash off the humiliating field-hand experience. Her hands had turned a greenish shade and dirt was caked under each fingernail. She scrubbed and scrubbed with an Avon product, but she wouldn't be able to scrub picking tomatoes from her memory.

Not that long ago, she had enjoyed the experiences in Georgia. It was hard to believe how quickly things had turned around. Foremost on her mind again was the desire to leave Fullerton and all of its trappings for good. She was just out of her element in the country.

33

Theo had informed his family that they were all going to church service the following Sunday. Ruby knew his real intent was to meet with the visiting minister, a Reverend Dr. Lawrence Wilson from an A.M.E. church in Pittsburgh, Pennsylvania. Ruby had not yet warmed up to the idea of baring her soul to a person of the cloth. To prevent Theo's sister from finding out about Madame Edwina's little bottle, and to keep a degree of sanity at home, she had not presented strong objections as long as Rev. Williams (the local pastor) would not be made privy to the matter to be discussed.

On the Sunday in question, the Mitchells headed for church, decked out in their Sunday clothes with Theo at the wheel. He was still sporting a cast. They certainly turned some heads when they approached a pew to be seated, because rarely did the congregation at Back Creek see the entire Mitchell family in church at the same time. Some nods of acknowledgement exchanged between Ruby and Theo and other adult parishioners. That was the polite way to greet once inside the sanctuary of their Methodist church. None of the parishioners who occasionally visited Theo's Place for a little libation acknowledged the family. A large dose of denial followed by a chaser of hypocrisy ordered their steps whenever they found themselves in a house of God.

Rev. Williams took his seat behind the lectern. A short stocky man with a burst of white fuzzy hair and a thick white mustache followed closely behind. He sat next to Rev. Williams. Ruby presumed him to be the guest minister. Service began as was usually the case at Back Creek with the Prelude followed by the Welcome, Call to Worship, etc. The first hymn performed was "Leaning on the Everlasting Arms." Eventually, "What a Friend we have in Jesus" and "We've Come This far by Faith" were sung. Rev. Williams' prayer was early in the program, and he opened with, "Lord, we humbly beseech you to look down upon your flock today and to help us stay on a holy path as we use scriptures inspired by you to guide us. Today is a special day for Back Creek. For we are truly honored that you have blessed us with the presence of Rev. Dr. Lawrence Wilson from Guiding Light A.M.E. Church in Pittsburgh, Pennsylvania. We know you sent Rev. Wilson to us, and we know all of us are in need of listening to the message he will bring. So this morning, church, I want you to open not only your ears but also your hearts and minds. Take heed to the message Dr. Wilson will deliver."

As Rev. Williams sat down, Rev. Wilson approached the pulpit and delivered a powerful message in a boisterous voice that defied his barely 5' stature. His message centered on what it takes to be redeemed in the eyes of God. Ruby felt like crumbling to the floor.

After the service ended, the girls ran back to the car, ready to get back home and rip off their stiff and starchy can-can slips and blouses. They wanted to focus on things important to kids, even Lindie—not the word delivered by a short stranger with fuzzy white hair. As they sat in the car waiting for their parents, they watched as Ruby and Theo greeted other parishioners who had gathered out on the church lawn. "I hope they hurry up. I'm bored, and it's hot." announced Francine.

"Not as hot as Alabama." Lindie was quietly wondering to herself why people had to huddle together after church as though they were just meeting for the first time. Most of them were neighbors and could have gossiped about whatever during the week. Most of them probably had telephones with party lines, so they could have group conversations in the comfort of their homes instead of standing under a blazing sun, sweating like beasts in their Sunday clothes. It just didn't make any sense to her. If they needed healing or a special prayer, they could appeal to and watch the televangelist, Oral Roberts. There had been times when Lindie heard him yell, *Heal*, while laying hands on those supposedly afflicted.

Ruby returned to the car, followed about 10 minutes later by her husband, who waited for the visiting minister to get in his car and follow them. Back at the house, Ruby told the girls to change into casual clothes and go outside and play until she called them. If they were caught back in the house before she said they could return, all three would have to answer to their father. Needless to say, that threat immediately brought back the tomato field experience that they did not want to repeat.

Rev. Wilson was offered a tall cold glass of lemonade, after which Theo provided some information as to why he and his wife wanted to talk with him privately. The reverend could not have been more gracious. "Let me assure you, this kind of thing is nothing new to me. I'm married myself, 25-years to the same woman, and Lord knows all the years have not been rosy. You share whatever you feel comfortable telling a stranger, but I won't be sharing anything you tell me with anybody else, because the advisor I listen to is . . ." He pointed upward, meaning God. "He's truly my best friend, my confidante, and my redeemer, because I'm a sinner just like all of his children on earth. I make mistakes, but I take it to God and ask for forgiveness. We all need forgiveness at one time or another. If we were intended to be without sin, then why did Christ have to die on the cross? Let's bow our heads for a prayer before you tell me more."

After the impassioned prayer, Theo went into more pointed details about his marriage. It took some prodding on the part of Rev. Wilson, but Ruby finally opened up and rendered a teary confession. All were emotionally and physically drained at the end of the session that was not devoid of harsh words and accusations. But, leaning on teachings from the good book and his personal experiences, Rev. Wilson did not allow the husband and wife to render personal attacks to the point of shutting down the meeting. The two-hour session ended after Rev. Wilson extracted a promise from both Ruby and Theo to try harder at re-establishing a close relationship and to get their priorities in order. He reminded them that tomorrow is promiscd to no one and that if God decides to catch them up short, there won't be time to get their house in order at the last minute. He promised to call them once a week for a progress report until he felt satisfied they were somewhat back on track as a normal married couple.

"Rev. you can't call us about this because we have a party line and don't want our neighbors in our business."

"Tell you what, I'll call but use a code and pretend I'm telling you about some members of my congregation and asking your opinions, but I want to speak with both of you. Else I'm going to ask you to confer with Rev. Williams or come to Pittsburgh and see me."

"We'll take yo' calls Reverend."

"Good. May the good Lord shine upon you both during this very trying time."

With that, the visiting pastor was off to meet Rev. Williams at the parsonage for dinner before returning to Pittsburgh.

34

The remaining lazy days of summer 1965 came and went without major incidents at the Mitchell household. Anything that resembled a ruckus was created by critters that buzzed, croaked, or made other natural sounds that routinely filled the air in most rural villages. Ruby and Theo didn't have any shouting matches, but they still were not warming up to each other— physically. It was as though both had resigned themselves to a passionless marriage in order to fulfil their primary responsibilities as mother and father to their three daughters.

Theo's cast was removed early, but it took several days for the coloring on his right arm to return to normal. He was ecstatic when an x-ray of his injured arm revealed that removal of the cast did not have to be delayed. Then he felt confident in spreading the word that he would need the assistance of at least one other person in order to get his firewood delivery enterprise fully up and running again. Soon, customers would be placing their orders for cords of seasoned wood in preparation for late fall and winter.

The relationship between Lindie and Theo remained as strong as it ever was, but Lindie's relationship with her mother was a work in progress. After all, the years when their relationship had been strained were not few in number.

It was Ruby's idea to replace the annual end of summer visit to the beach with a drive through Shenandoah Valley. Theo did not offer any opposition, not even after Ruby invited Fred and his family along. However, the kids were not thrilled about a ride through the mountains. How much fun could that possibly be compared to frolicking half naked in neck-high water with other kids whom they looked forward to seeing each summer? But, the decision had been made. Just as the beach outings had been, the drive through the mountains would also be a single day away from routine activities. Ruby and Barbara decided on the food they'd have for a picnic to be enjoyed at the end of the drive.

The Mitchell girls, more so than their Philly cousins, showed an extreme lack of enthusiasm for the trip to Shenandoah Valley. During one of the girls' trips into town with their mother, Francine asked if they could spend some time at the public library. It was there that she asked the reference librarian for some information on Shenandoah Valley. She had hoped to find next to nothing, and to therefore mount an argument against the trip. To her surprise the librarian found tons of information. Francine left the library armed with two books filled with color photos of

Shenandoah National Park. Flipping through the pages with her sisters did lift their interest a bit. Lindie remembered reading in one of their encyclopedias before the fire that there were Virginia plantations with slaves in parts of Shenandoah Valley. She shared this with her sisters and also asked their mother if they would be seeing any plantations while in Virginia.

"We're just driving through a portion of the valley and stopping at some lookout points-- not stopping off to explore any slave history and certainly not to set foot on a plantation."

"But it's history, Momma."

"I don't care what it is, the answer is no."

Nor was Theo making any plans for the trip. After cutting the front lawn one day, he was in the process of cutting back a tea rose bush that was beginning to crowd out some smaller flowering plants. He was still working in the yard when the mail was delivered. He collected the mail, fully expecting everything to be addressed to either himself or Ruby, so he was surprised to find a postcard addressed to Lindie.

Everyone knows (even if they won't admit it) it's hard to resist reading messages scrawled on the back of post cards even when they are addressed to others. There was a Georgia postmark on the card, so Theo's interest was piqued since Georgia had been one of Lindie's stops during her visit south. At first he was poised to just deliver the card to Lindie, thinking it was likely from Marlene's kids asking how she was doing.

But curiosity got the best of him when his eyes zoomed in on the signature. The signature on the card read Calvin. The message was, "Dear Lindie, such a pretty name for a pretty girl. I wanted to write earlier but didn't for some reason. I'm letting you know again that I enjoyed our slow dance, and if you ever visit Georgia again, please let me know. Another dance and more awaits."

Theo immediately thought to himself, *the hell?* Lots of other thoughts came to mind, but utmost was his assumption that once again Lindie was keeping a secret. He shut off the lawn mower and sat down in a shaded spot to ponder the possible impact of confronting her and asking who the hell Calvin was. She had not mentioned his name when she recounted her visit south —several other names, but nothing about a Calvin as far as he could remember. Then he considered how his wife would likely react if she were to see the post card. He reminded himself that Lindie would be turning 12 soon. He stood up, shoved the post card in his back pocket, and made swift work of finishing up his yard chores.

Lindie was relaxing in her bedroom listening to records being spun by disc jockey Hoppy Adams on WANN out of Annapolis. *I Want a Love I can See* by the Temptations was playing. Her journal was within reach because she had spent some time that morning adding to her entries about what she had experienced down south. At that point the recollections she recorded focused upon things related to race. She wrote about the insulting rhyme uttered by the person in South Carolina and the mother in Maryland who didn't want her child to sit close to her and her aunt. The memory of Ricky's closet full of guns still made her shiver. However, most of her entries about her trip south had to do with the four civil rights workers who were tortured and killed in Mississippi and the mother from Detroit who was shot in the head while driving her car—all killed by a hate group called the Klu Klux Klan.

Theo returned to the house, still undecided about how to deal with what he had read on the postcard. He found Ruby ironing clothes in the kitchen while pots were cooking away on the stove with whatever she was preparing for supper that evening. Smelled like chicken and dumplings to him.

"I think we need to call Lindie to the tavern only when you really need help. She's almost 12, and some of them men who come in the place might start payin' too much attention to her. We ain't got eyes in the back of our heads, and can't see every-thin' that goes on in front of us either."

"I had come to that conclusion too. You can tell her we don't need her tonight, but when I fix food for the picnic, I will need her help."

"That's fine. I might think 'bout puttin' up a door wid a latch at the kitchen entrance."

"You trying to keep me in or somebody out?" teased Ruby.

Theo shrugged his shoulders and said, "Just think it's the right thing to do."

Theo went to his bedroom and sat on the bed thinking more about what he had read on the postcard. He thought back over the few things Lindie had shared about her trip, but mostly he remembered the tears she had shed—tears that touched his heart because he had advocated for letting her go on the trip. The tears signaled that she didn't want to come back home. Had he missed something? Now he desperately wanted to know what the queen of secrets had not shared, and he thought he had the perfect way to find out. He removed his work clothes and threw them in a hamper before changing into a pair of khakis and a casual shirt.

First he rounded up his youngest two, and then he knocked on Lindie's door where he found her still listening to WANN. She was also dancing to the music instead of writing as he had presumed she was doing.

"Ya'll wanna go to Dairy Queen for ice cream cones?"

Shouts of delight erupted from Francine and Vinnie while Lindie seemed more lukewarm about the offer.

"Fine with me, but can I get a banana split instead of a cone?" asked Lindie.

"We see when we get there. I'm pullin' out in five minutes."

Theo walked into the kitchen and told Ruby he was taking the girls to town for ice cream. She didn't mount too much of a protest, only stated that it would be better for dessert after dinner, but he would be getting them out of her way for a while. She continued with her household chores.

The banana split was humongous. Francine and Vinnie settled for small vanilla cones dipped in chocolate. Theo opted for a coke, all of which was enjoyed as the four of them sat in the car in the shaded spot where Theo had parked.

"So, you girls all ready for a new school year?"

"I am cause I'm anxious to finish elementary school," declared Francine.

"I'm not cause I like playing around the house, and the bus is cold in the winter," shared Vinnie.

"And you, Ms. Lindie?"

"I guess, but 8th grade is going to be harder than 7th and probably a lot more work. I do hope I can give a report about the south in my history class."

"Speakin' of the south, you didn't give up much information, mostly cried when we left Philly. What have you left out? Did you meet some kids your age, go any special places?"

"I told you all about the two girls I met at a pastor's house in Birmingham and the thunderstorm I got caught in. I also told you about Aunt Barbara's sister and her kids—one older than me and two younger."

"Really, what was their names?"

"Reggie's the oldest, and the younger two are Paul and Andrea."

"Anybody else?"

Lindie shook her head, "Not worth mentioning. Aunt Barbara's sister and her husband have a nice home, and I was offered watermelon when we first arrived."

"You don't like watermelon," reminded Francine.

"No I don't, but I remembered my manners and ate as much as I could."

"That's it?" asked her father.

"Except I'd like to go back to Georgia. Fort Sierra was like a big city with lots to do. Maybe I'll marry an army man one day." Lindie giggled as her father struggled to find an appropriate response.

"You don't say . . . well, I ain't heard Barbara say anythin' 'bout goin' back next year, 'sides by then you might have changed your mind."

"I'm sure I won't change my mind. Georgia was special."

"I see."

With their midday treats consumed, Theo drove back home, and on the way he informed Lindie she would be spending less time in the tavern. He also told her about the door he might install at the kitchen entrance in order to keep eager customers from bothering her mother while she's working.

"That's a good idea, Daddy. A couple of weeks ago when I was helping Momma in the kitchen, I turned around and a customer was staring at me and sticking out his tongue. I just ignored him."

Theo tightened his grip on the steering wheel. "Glad you told me that baby girl." He knew then that the door would be an immediate addition as soon as they returned from Shenandoah Valley. He also knew if Ruby put up any opposition later on, he'd tell her what Lindie had just shared, but the postcard—he didn't think so.

Ruby assigned all three girls chores when they returned home. Vinnie was learning to wash dishes. Francine had to help hang clothes on the clothesline, and Lindie had to round up the remaining dirty items from all bedrooms and the bathroom for washing. She cleaned out the bathroom first; then she pulled sheets from the bedroom shared by her sisters. Her room had already been cleaned. Finally she went to her parents' bedroom, pulled the dirty sheets, made up the bed with clean sheets, and emptied the hamper. While gathering clothes from the hamper, a post card fell to the floor. It landed front-side up revealing an aerial shot of Fort Sierra. She quickly scooped up the card and flipped it over. Her mouth flew open, and her eyes bulged when she saw it had been signed by Calvin. She closed the door to the bedroom and quickly read the message. Then she sat down on the edge of the bed and tried to gather her thoughts, of which there were many, mostly in the form of questions. She looked at the clothes still gathered in her arms, and they all belonged to her father.

Daddy must have taken this out of the mailbox and read it? She quickly checked the hamper for more mail, but nothing more— just the post card. *Why did Calvin write me and how did he get my address? I didn't ask him to write me . . . did I?* After all, she was nearly in a state of delirium as her last evening in Georgia came to an end. *Is that why Daddy was asking me more about my trip when we were at the Dairy Queen? What do I do?* As much as she wanted to keep the card, she knew she couldn't, so she ran to her room and grabbed a piece of paper and pencil to write down Calvin's address. Then she ripped the card into tiny pieces and stuffed them back into a pocket on her father's pants. *Let the washing machine destroy it.* Not waiting for her mother, Lindie dumped a bundle of clothes into the washing machine along with detergent and started a cycle. She would pretend she had not found the card.

At dinner that evening Theo brought it up, and Lindie thought she was going to have to bolt from the table, but quick thinking saved her.

"Ruby, did you wash all the dirty clothes I had in the hamper?"

"I guess so. Ask Lindie. She's the one who cleaned up our room and emptied the hamper. Why?"

"I think I misplaced somethin'. Thought maybe it ended up in the hamper."

"Did you find something in your father's clothes?"

What can I say that's not a lie? "I just grabbed up a bundle of clothes along with the sheets, loaded the machine, and started the cycle."

"Then whatever you think you lost, you must 'a put it somewhere else . . . Oh, I did find some shreds of paper in the bottom of the machine, but it just looked like soggy trash that I often find in your clothes because you never empty your pockets before putting clothes in the hamper." Lindie was nearly unglued by the time Ruby finished her explanation about the debris in the washer.

Theo's eyes were burning beams at Lindie, and she could feel his glare. She shot a quick glance at him, and his glare immediately switched to an expression that could have passed for a knowing smile. Her knees were knocking under the table and she suddenly lost her appetite. She claimed a sudden onset of stomach pain and retreated to her bedroom. Ruby assumed cramps possibly.

Lindie did not look at her father as she left the dinner table, but once she was out of sight, Ruby said to Theo, "It's probably a female thing."

Once inside her bedroom, Lindie fell to her knees, not in confession but panic instead. Now she knew for sure why her father had asked those questions at the Dairy Queen. He had not shown it to her mother because she certainly would have confronted her. *What is he planning to do? Why did you write me Calvin?* She grabbed each side of her head and pulled on her hair in frustration. Then there was a knock at her door.

"Can I come in?" It was her father.

Quickly she got under the covers of her bed in order to solidify her claim of not feeling well.

"Come in."

Theo sat on the corner of Lindie's bed, but she had not worked up the nerve to look him in the face.

"Not feelin' well?"

"Umm, umm, but I'll be better after I rest a little bit."

Theo laughed to himself, but didn't want to prolong what he intended to do.

"We gonna play this back and forth game, or are you gonna tell me that you saw the post card?"

Lindie bolted straight up in her bed. "Daddy, I didn't tell him to write me. I promise I didn't."

"I'm more concerned 'bout this slow dance. What you got to say 'bout that? Was you alone wid this Calvin?"

"No Daddy, it wasn't like that at all. On the last night Aunt Barbara and I were in Georgia, a friend of one of Ms. Marlene's sons invited us to a party. Both Aunt Barbara and Ms. Marlene said it was okay for me to go."

"Was any adults at this party?"

"Yes, it was at Calvin's home, and his parents were there. His father is an officer, and they live in a nice big house a little ways from Ms. Marlene."

"So how is it you ended up doin' a slow dance wid Calvin? How old is he?"

He's . . . maybe four years older than me, and when the song came on, I guess he felt sorry for me. I was a guest."

"So he offered you a pity dance?"

"I don't know, Daddy. You're making a big deal out of nothing —one dance; that's all it was—no bear-hug dancing like customers do in the tavern."

"But this party and the slow dance skipped yo' mind when you was tellin' us 'bout yo' trip."

Lindie had no response to offer to that statement; only to ask, "You didn't tell Momma about the post card did you?"

"You ain't got 'nother sore arm do you? You almost 12, Lindie, and boys are gonna be payin' more attention to you. I know yo' momma has already talked to you 'bout the birds and the bees, so I ain't gonna get into that, but I will say you got to carry yo' self wid respect. If you don't respect yo' self, ain't nobody gonna respect you. Momma and Daddy ain't gonna be able to jump in and protect you ever' time trouble might be lurkin'. You got to be smart."

Lindie relaxed her pensive composure, thinking the interrogation was over when her father got up from her bed to leave, but then he didn't leave.

"I'm gonna leave you wid some thoughts. You might think I'm just an old man talkin' nonsense, but hear me good. First, I been livin' a lot of years, and I know how holdin' back information and deceitful acts can reach back and hurt people, even if hurt wasn't intended. Second, you might have a few experiences in yo' life that should remain secret if tellin' the truth is gonna hurt somebody, but that can get real ugly dependin' upon the situation. I hope any experiences like that for you will be few, cause hurts caused by lies and deceit can't always be healed. And third, don't ever do anythin' you're gonna be ashamed of later." After delivering those lines of wisdom, Theo looked at his daughter and let his stare linger for a couple of seconds as he waited to see if she had anything additional to share, but she didn't. He had a look upon his face that she could not read with any degree of certainty. Then he left her room and gently closed her door.

Lindie swung her feet to the floor but remained seated on her bed as she thought about everything her father had just said. After going back over his words a couple of times, she didn't understand why his finding out about her simple, slow dance had sparked such warnings. She decided that only time would reveal whatever he was really talking about, but she would write Calvin and tell him not to write again until she turned 16.

After the trip through Shenandoah Valley, Lindie intended to finish out the rest of summer break reviewing the journal notes she had taken while in the south and drafting an outline for a report. She felt she had enough information to share should an opportunity be presented in her next history class.

As she was correcting her outline two days before the new school year started, her mother interrupted her concentration.

"I'm going into town. Wanna go with me?"

"Are my sisters going also?"

"No, just you and me. Plus I made an appointment with a beautician for you to get your hair done."

"For real!"

"Yes, so hurry up and get ready."

Lindie tossed her papers aside, hastily pulled her hair into a ponytail, and checked her appearance in a mirror before joining her mother at the car. She was sort of pleased with her appearance. She had grown a bit taller over the summer. Most importantly she now had boobies that finally stood to attention under her blouse. Getting her hair done by a beautician would be the icing on the cake after the best summer she'd ever had.

Author Bio

Ann Bayah was born and reared on Maryland's Eastern Shore. Ms. Bayah's love of putting pen to paper started when she was barely old enough to understand the power of the written word. Her mother introduced her to poetry and prose at an early age, and thus, served as the author's primary inspiration for writing. In addition to her mother's influence, Ms. Bayah's writings are impacted by myriad other influences, stemming back to life on the Eastern Shore and beyond. She never considered writing as a career option, but after completing her post graduate work, she toyed with the idea of writing prose, plays, poetry, and short stories as an avocation. From the time she received the stunning news that she had won a statewide play writing contest, she began to dream of producing a novel one day. Ms. Bayah is still a Maryland resident.

"First they ignore you, then they laugh
at you, then they fight you, then you win."

Mahatma Gandhi

www.ingramcontent.com/pod-product-compliance
Lightning Source LLC
Chambersburg PA
CBHW050042180626
46810CB00002B/847